D1714852

WITHIN
THE PALACE GATES

The Story of Nehemiah
Cupbearer to King Artaxerxes

BY

ANNA PIERPONT SIVITER

Illustrated

W. A. WILDE COMPANY
PUBLISHERS   BOSTON

Cover art: James Converse
Cover design: Chrystique Neibauer
Copyright: 1992

A.B. Publishing, Inc.
3039 S Bagley
Ithaca, Mi 48847
www.abpub.com

FOREWORD

IN the middle of the last century archæologists brought to light, at Susa, in Persia, the palace of Shushan, and the civilized world thrilled to the description of its great size and magnificence. Then attention was directed to other wonders of ancient civilization which the spades of scientific investigators have ever since been upturning in Oriental lands.

As the author of "Within the Palace Gates" followed the endless succession of these discoveries, especially the more recent ones of the citadel of the palace at Susa, there came to her a keen desire to re-people the Persian city with its ancient inhabitants. Their wars and religion, their dress, food, customs, homes, furniture, laws and punishments, were all depicted clearly and accurately, but what of the men and women themselves? What were their ideals, education, ambitions, loves and hates?

To learn more of them she turned to the pages of Herodotus, Xenophon, Ezra and Josephus, and to modern archæologists, Ferguson, Rawlinson, Loftus and de Morgan; and, most helpful of all, to the history of two persons who had lived in thispalace— one the wife of a great king, a dramatic episode written by a contemporary; and the other the diary of a favorite, the cup-bearer of King Artaxerxes. From all these authorities the history of the king's cup-bearer was built—a story whose setting the author believes is absolutely accurate, and many of whose characters are historical, as well as its main events. It is given to the public in the hope that it may help others to reconstruct the life of the people of those days, who lived more than two thousand years ago.

ANNA PIERPONT SIVITER.

WITHIN
THE PALACE GATES

The Story of Nehemiah,
Cupbearer to King Artaxerxes

╋╋

CHAPTER I

THE day had been hot and sultry, but as darkness
fell over the plains of Persia, a pitying breeze
sprang up in the mountains of Luristan, and, gliding
down their rugged sides, hidden now under a wealth
of rhododendron and wild almond blossoms, it had
dipped its wings in the clear, cool waters of the river
Choaspes.

Then, sweeping over the Susianian plains, through
orchards of peach and apple, orange and lemon trees,
it caught all the fragrance of their pink and white
blossoms, and, mingling them in one delicious odor,
was carrying its cool sweetness to the inhabitants of
Susa, — Susa, city of lilies, home and capital of the
great king, Artaxerxes Longimanus.

Very fair the city looked, as it shone in the last rays
of the setting sun, to a body of travellers whose cara-

van was slowly moving through the orchards and wheat fields toward it. Its huge brick walls, towering fifty feet in the air, hid the homes of the poorer citizens; but they were broken down in many places, and the city, pouring through them, had spread its handsome red and pink and buff brick houses for many miles around, and now these, surrounded by lovely gardens, seemed to the approaching travellers to be only a sample of the beauty and grandeur the city contained.

As the travellers neared the entrance to Susa, more than once a cry of admiration escaped them. Early in the afternoon they had seen what seemed to be a beautiful cloud hovering over the city; but as they came nearer, it took form and shape, until the slanting rays of the sinking sun brought out in all its magnificence the palace and treasure house, fortress and home, of the richest and most powerful ruler in the world, — "Artaxerxes, King of Kings," as he proudly emblazoned himself in imperishable letters on the palace gates, "Son of Darius, Lord of Lords, Ruler of the Earth and Sea."

How wonderfully magnificent the palace was, as it lifted itself from the flower-decked plain below into the sunset clouds two hundred feet above! It looked as if it had stolen from them their beautiful tints, and was holding them prisoned on its lofty columns, its wide porticoes, its massive walls; for crimson and gold and purple, violet, orange, and blue, — all the colors the mighty sun can paint, when he hangs his most gorgeous tapestries against the western sky, — were here on this building, the wonder of the ages, Shushan the palace.

As the caravan plodded along, one of the travellers, who was riding a handsome horse, turned to a sad-faced man who rode beside him, half supporting in his arms a clinging, childish figure.

"It is no wonder," said the first, addressing his companion, "that the great Darius chose this lovely spot on which to build himself a city, where he could find security and rest. Methinks had he searched the world over he would not have found a place more pleasant to the eye."

"It is very beautiful, my Lord Asshur," the traveller answered. "Know you if King Artaxerxes is there now?"

"Yes; I questioned the guards at the mountain pass as we came through, and they told me the king, with his court, had taken up his residence there for the remainder of the year, and to-morrow he will receive tribute in yon palace. Have you brought aught with you?"

"I have this ass I am leading," the traveller answered. "It is snow-white, without spot or blemish, such as our own kings once rode upon. I have trained it myself, and know it is gentle, and yet speedy enough for the use of a courier of the king."

"It is a fitting present," Asshur said, turning to look at the animal, which was pacing along beside the camel the traveller was riding. "The king himself may ride it, on some hunting expedition." And he gazed again approvingly at the ass.

Asshur was a tall, dark man, dressed in the Persian fashion, and the traveller recognized in him the familiar figure of a tribute-gatherer of the king. He had a kindly face, and as he glanced at the man riding beside him, tenderly holding the child, his look softened, and he said: —

"You have come a long distance, have you not, my friend? I remember your camel joined my caravan at the head of the desert. Have you friends in Susa? Know you where you will rest to-night? The child seems very weary."

"He is weary," the traveller replied, "and we are strangers in Susa. It is to make petition of the king I have come hither."

"Then you shall go with us," a young man cried, who was riding beside the tribute-gatherer. "Come,

Asshur, there is plenty of room in the palace for the boy and his father. Ever since I joined you at the mountain pass, the little lad has been laying siege to my heart with his gentle words and laughing eyes."

"Your heart is never very hard to take, is it, Adna, whether maid or child lay siege to it?" Asshur laughed. "But if thy master my Lord Nehe does not complain, I shall not, and the travellers can enter the palace with my escort."

"That settles it, then," Adna cried, his handsome face glowing with pleasure. "You can remain in the garden when we have entered the city, until I make provision for you within the palace walls. But have no fear; there is room and to spare, even when the fortress holds its thousands and tens of thousands, as it will to-night."

"Is there so great a company, then?" Asshur asked, turning to the young man.

"Indeed there is," he answered. "Not only will the king receive tribute to-morrow, but he will also receive ambassadors from Greece, who have come to arrange a peace for Egypt. But I shall make room for you and the child," he added, again turning to the stranger, "in my own chamber."

"I thank you many times," the traveller responded. "Surely we shall be well provided for."

And he looked gratefully at the graceful young rider, whose rich coat of burnished mail showed he belonged to the king's own household; and the shadow lifted from his saddened face as they rode on. Just as the sun dropped out of sight he passed, with the caravan, over the moat and through the gate of the outer wall that encircled the palace and its gardens. Here, instructed by Adna, he dismounted, and awaited a summons into the palace itself.

As the night fell, another inmate of the palace had come down into the stillness and sweetness of the garden. He was a young man, and as he passed down the staircase whose gentle descent gleamed like a river of polished silver in the light of the many torches that the torch-bearers were already holding, the scarlet-kilted soldiers standing guard had lowered their long spears respectfully, and forbore to challenge him, for they recognized, even in that light, that he was no less a personage than Nehe, the cup-bearer and favorite of the king.

At first he had strolled idly among the lily-beds, stopping sometimes to break off a tall, white flower, or to glance up at the palace that towered above him in the moonlight. Snatches of a sweet, plaintive song came from the harem garden, that nestled against the palace walls, and Nehe stopped occasionally to listen, as the notes floated out on the night air, and he smiled, recognizing the clear, girlish voice as that of Lydia, his mother's own handmaiden.

The silken curtains of the banqueting-rooms of the palace had been looped back, and as the lights in their large hanging lamps were lit, the buildings glowed with light and color. Afar across the plains, answering gleams shot up from the mountain height, and Nehe sighed as he saw them. He knew they came from the altar fires built by the faithful Persian priests high on the mountain tops, and he wondered why this people should be so much more faithful to the worship of their god than his own had been. With a slight gesture of impatience he turned his back on the palace and mountain, and walked farther down into the garden, until he reached a clump of acacia trees that shut him from view. The darkness hid the clusters of pink blossoms that were softly swaying among the trees' feathery foliage, but their sweetness betrayed them.

Here Nehe stopped, drawing in deep breaths and smiling up at the flowers in the shadows. He seemed a fitting inhabitant of that fair garden as he stood there. The moonlight sifting through the acacias' plumes showed an uplifted, beautiful, but almost boyish face, crowned with clustering black curls, and bound around with a fillet of gold, set with a single glittering stone that shone like a star in the moonlight. His dress was a white silk robe, so closely fitting about the neck and chest that it showed the splendid proportions of its wearer. A golden girdle confined it at the waist, and long, tapering, yellow shoes, buttoned with gems, completed his costume.

Suddenly a nightingale in the boughs above him burst into song, as if it, too, felt all the quiet beauty of the night, and, catching the perfume of the flowers, the plash of the fountain, the play of the breeze, it wrapped them all in notes of exquisite sweetness, and was sending forth its song, an offering to the Creator of the eve. As the song trilled out, Nehe smiled again more joyously.

"Bird," he said aloud, and his voice, as he spoke, had cadences as sweet to the human ear as those of the feathered songster whose music was pulsing around him, "bird, sing me the song of my fortune! See," and he lifted up his strong right hand and looked at its rosy palm, "so long as this guards the cup of my lord the king, I shall be rich and proud and happy."

Then he turned the bracelet that encircled his wrist, and looked intently at the beautiful gem with which it was set, and smiled again as he recalled how gracious the king had been when he gave it to him that day.

"Come, my Nehe," he had said, "here are the gems just sent me as tribute by the Egyptians. You shall have your choice. The queen mother and Damaspia have sent me word they would have choice of them, but," and the monarch had smiled a haughty, good-natured smile, "lest they should choose this, we will ourself bestow it on you. I know you will prize it." And, lifting the bracelet, he had handed it to Nehe, adding as he did so, "The gem, you see, is curiously engraved, even with the countenance of an Egyptian king."

But as Nehe stood looking at it there in the silvery moonlight, a shadow crossed his bright face and his white teeth bit into his red lips with a sigh of sudden pain, for Nehe remembered that as he had bent in thanks before the king, his eyes had fallen on the face of a nobleman standing near, whose lips were curled in a bitter, supercilious smile. The man had been a former favorite of the king, but of late had fallen under the monarch's displeasure, and so was keeping himself as much as possible out of sight; but, unfortunately for him, just then the king turned suddenly to speak to his fan-bearer, and he, too, caught the malicious gleam of the noble's dark eyes and the scornful curl of his lips. The good-natured look left his face, and one of keen displeasure replaced it. "And do you scorn the king's cup-bearer for having won his master's favor, Zexa?" he said; "or is it the king himself you scorn?" Then, turning to the attendants standing near, he said angrily, "Away with him! Let me see his face no more."

The trembling man flung himself before the throne with a fearful cry.

"Mercy, my lord, mercy!" he moaned. "'Twas but a sudden twinge of pain did distort my countenance."

"Your pains come too often, Zexa," the king replied, sternly; "and Persian kings alter not their words. I have said it. To the death!"

Two attendants seized the man and bore him rapidly from the royal presence, and as Nehe remembered the unfortunate noble's look of agony he moved rapidly from the acacia tree, as if he would fly from the memory of the scene.

And yet in spite of his cruelty, Nehe truly loved the great and terrible Artaxerxes, for he had been kind and even indulgent to him; and though the young courtier was just entering manhood, he was already one of the richest and most influential men of the Persian court. So great a favorite was he with his royal master that the king frequently sought and was guided by Nehe's advice in matters of state, and he felt that a great future lay before him.

Persia was at the zenith of her power. All the nations of the known world had seen her hand of steel held out to them, and none had refused to lay in it of her most priceless treasures. Egypt itself, possessor of untold wealth, was now a vassal; and even the sturdy little nation of Greece, intrenched behind its barriers of mountain and sea, did not refuse to allow its continental cities to send tribute to the great Persian. It was not strange then, as Nehe walked there in the flower-scented garden, visions floated before him of honor and wealth and happiness that the future surely held for him. Perhaps he would become a great general and extend still farther the Persian boundaries. The great Cyrus had found new worlds to conquer; who knew what mighty empires he might find lying far across the mountains? Perhaps — and he involuntarily took a step forward — the old legend was true, and there was a beautiful land far beyond the green waters of the great Pontus.

As he did so he inadvertently ran against a little boy who was passing, and knocked him down. Nehe stopped, picked the little fellow up, and as he set him on his feet again, he said gently: —

"Hush you, my lad! Where is your father? Does he not know better than to let you run loose in the king's garden?"

"Here, my lord," said a man, stepping from the shadow of a tall palm, and catching the sobbing boy in his arms. "If we are trespassing, I beg my lord's pardon, and we will hasten away. I have but lately come to this country, and the city is strange to me. I knew not we were on forbidden ground."

"From whence came you?" Nehe inquired, looking closely at the travel-worn garments of the stranger. "No citizen of Susa but knows there be many safer places to walk than in the garden of the king."

"My lord," answered the man, eagerly, apparently frightened at Nehe's stern tone, "we be from Jerusalem, one of the least of the far-away cities belonging to his Majesty, the great king, and we know not yet what is expected of the citizens of Susa; but, my lord, from henceforth no lovely garden and green walks shall tempt us to loiter."

"Wisely said, O stranger from Jerusalem," answered the young man; "but tell me, if you are Jews, and from Jerusalem, how goes it in that far-off country?"

"Badly enough," answered the stranger, sadly

"Our city, once the pride and hope of a great nation, lies now at the mercy of her enemies. Her mighty walls, that towered toward heaven and made us laugh at our foes, have been broken down, and her children, like chickens unsheltered by the brooding wings of their mother, are at the mercy of every cruel inhabitant of the land."

"True," said Nehe, "a city without walls is very helpless; and have you yourself suffered, good sir?"

"I!" exclaimed the man, bitterly; "I! Alas, what have I not suffered? When I was but a child I lived with my father and mother and little brother in one of the small towns that nestled at the foot of the great walls of Jerusalem. Once it was safe enough to live there, for the watchman standing above gave warning if any danger threatened. Then, although the walls were broken down, we were lulled into a false sense of security because the great king had allowed many of our people to return from captivity and to begin rebuilding our temple, and we thought his protection would keep us safe from molestation; but, alas! one day a party of Samaritans, sent by our enemy, Sanballat, came sweeping up the valley.

"My parents saw them coming, and might have escaped, but they delayed their flight, trying to hide me, for I was ill of a fever, and they thought me dying. They knew to try to move me far meant certain death, and so with loving haste they carried me into the barn and hid me in a pile of flax. Just then the Samaritans entered. Alas! I can even now hear my mother's shriek as the fierce, dark men seized her and my baby brother, who was clinging to her skirts, and bore them and my father, struggling, away."

"Did you never see them again?" Nehe asked, in a sympathetic tone.

"Never," the stranger answered. "For many weeks I lay in a stupor, but thanks to the loving care of our faithful servant Joro, I at last recovered."

"Joro?" questioned Nehe, in a startled tone. "'Tis an odd name, and yet methinks I have heard it before."

"It was not his real name," was the reply. "My baby brother gave it to him, trying in vain to say Joram. We all took the name the baby called him, and so, though to strangers he was Joram, to me he was ever Joro."

"I see," said Nehe; "go on with your tale. It interests me strangely. Have you a thought where your father and mother and this baby brother may be?"

"I have spent many hours dreaming of them," the stranger answered, sadly. "Perhaps they were kept as slaves by the Samaritans. Perhaps they were sold to some passing caravan. They may have been sent to work in the brickyards of Egypt. They may even have been brought to this beautiful land of Persia. My father had rare skill as a gardener; my mother, Sarai, had as great as a weaver, and she was wondrous dexterous, too, with her needle. She it was who had been chosen by Ezra to embroider the veil for the new temple."

"Your mother's name was Sarai?" questioned Nehe; and the moonlight showed that his face had suddenly grown white as marble, while his eyes were glowing like coals with the intensity of some hidden feeling.

"Yes, her name was Sarai," the stranger answered, "and my father's name was Hachaliah. My own name is Hanani."

"Hachaliah! Hanani!" breathed Nehe, bending forward. "Go on, I pray you! How did you live alone?"

"Joram, the servant, brought me up, and tenderly and carefully instructed me in the religion of my fathers. A hard and a sad boyhood I had, however, for our enemies were ever ready to seize our crops and stock. Many a year, just when our grain was ready to thresh, have we seen them coming riding their swift horses like vultures; and almost before we realized they were near, they had trampled our fields and were gone, driving our cattle before them, and leaving us nothing for our winter's provision."

"And had you friends then who helped you?" Nehe asked.

"Oh, yes; all the citizens of Jerusalem were ready enough to share with one another. A common love, a common hatred, united us."

"And what was that?" Nehe asked.

"The worship of the Lord God Jehovah," the stranger answered, reverently looking up to the sky, "and the hatred of heathen gods."

"Are you not bold over much?" young Nehe asked, "to say that to me, here in the city of Susa, where a thousand gods do daily have prayer made unto them?"

"I crave your pardon, my lord," the stranger answered, hastily; "it seemed in speaking to you as if I spoke to one of our own nation. Will you let us pass on lest other words offend you?"

"No, no, my friend, I was not offended; go on with your tale and let me know why you came here."

"I came on a sorrowful errand, my lord. Among those who most befriended me after my father, mother, and little brother had been carried captive, was a goldsmith and perfume-maker, Hashum by name, and many and many a time, when we knew our home was in danger, have I taken refuge under his strong roof. One beautiful daughter he had, Hannah, and her, when I was grown to be a man, Hashum gave to me to be my wife. And then it was I first knew happiness. We had a little home, and for a few years most of the Arabs and other of our enemies were away in Artaxerxes' armies; so we tilled our fields in peace, and when two boys were born to us, Jamin, my first born, and Bani, this my baby, life seemed very good to me." And he drew the little fellow he was still holding more closely to him.

"I am hungry, father," the child said, aroused by the caress from a half sleep into which he had fallen; "hungry, and, so thirsty. Can I have some water?"

Nehe, who continued to drink in the stranger's words with intense eagerness, had advanced step by step toward him, as if he feared to lose even a syllable; but at the child's words his face lost a trifle of its intensity, and his eyes softened. Taking a silver whistle from his belt, he blew it. Instantly a young man, clad in yellow silk garments, came swiftly out of the shrubbery toward him, and, bowing low, stood awaiting his orders; and the stranger recognized, in spite of his changed costume, the youth Adna, who had brought them into the garden.

"Is this you, Adna?" Nehe exclaimed. "I thought that Daniel was in attendance to-night. When did you return from the mountains?"

"Scarce an hour since, my lord," replied Adna, "and I begged to wait upon you in Daniel's room, for I had a boon to ask."

"I will hear your request another time," Nehe said, impatiently. "I have other business for you now. Here, take this child to my apartments, give him honey and milk, pomegranates and grapes, and when he is refreshed, lay him in my own bed." Then, turning to the boy, he said, "Will you go and get the honey and milk, my child? And, Adna," he added, "mark you, tend him well, for he is my beloved nephew."

Then Nehe turned to the stranger and caught both his hands in his own.

"You are Hanani," he cried. "I am Nehemiah your brother."

CHAPTER II

A S Adna lifted the child from the ground and bore him smilingly away, the boy looked over his shoulder and saw his father lean eagerly forward as, almost incoherent with joy, he exclaimed:

"Now, God be praised! Oh, my brother, tell me, do my mother and father live?"

"Our father sleeps," Lord Nehe replied, softly. "He died a year ago."

"Only a year?" Hanani echoed, sorrowfully. "And I have mourned him since a child! I never hoped to see him, but Joram taught me to pray that our God would have him in his keeping."

"Your prayer was granted," Lord Nehe answered, softly, "But stop here by this light. I would see your face more clearly."

"Yes, yes," Hanani assented, almost impatiently, "but tell me, does my mother live?"

"Yes," Lord Nehe answered; "but I would see your face." And he turned and gazed long and searchingly at Hanani; then asserted: "Yes, there is no mistake, my brother. You have my father's eyes

27

and his mouth, and," he added, looking at his strong, graceful figure, "you carry yourself as he did, too. If he could only have seen this day!"

Hanani sighed, then eagerly questioned:—

"But my mother; what of her?"

Nehe answered:—

"Her joy will be very great this night, for she lives in the palace, honored and respected."

"I thank my God again," Hanani said, softly and reverently. "All my life Joram has kept her sweetness in my memory. And I shall see her tonight, my brother?"

His questioning voice was singularly like Lord Nehe's as he almost whispered the words "my brother."

"Yes, you shall see her tonight," Lord Nehe promised. "But first we must go to my apartment and see to little Bani; then get some food and send our mother word. And as we walk, tell me what brought you here, and why did you come."

"That is soon told," replied Hanani. "Five months ago I took little Bani for a day with his grandparents in Jerusalem. While we were gone a band of Philistines, led by the cruel Sanballat, swept down on my little home, just as they had done on that of my father. The news of the raid spread rapidly, and I rushed home, but Hannah and Jamin were gone. Bani was with me in the city, and he was saved."

"And have you had no tidings of them since?" Nehe asked. "My poor brother, how you have suffered!"

"No, I never even heard of them again, but faithful old Joram, who lived with us, told me that as a fierce Samaritan rode off with Hannah, she raised her beautiful eyes to heaven and pointed upward, as if she were telling him where to look for help."

"Did you make no effort to find her?" Nehe asked impatiently. "I would have searched desert and sea."

"My brother, how far do you think a single man could venture into the land of the Samaritans, no matter how well armed he might be, or how far could he go alone into the desert? But I did spend my little all in trying to bribe Sanballat to return my wife, only to be laughed to scorn in the end. He even denied all knowledge of her capture. Then it was that my father-in-law, the goldsmith, urged me to come to Susa and beseech the great king, Artaxerxes, to allow us, his faithful Jewish subjects, to rebuild the walls of our city, and so protect our loved ones from the cruel hordes who roam that country; for, though the king's great-grandfather, Cyrus, and his father, Xerxes, had allowed us to rebuild our beautiful

temple, our walls are still rubbish heaps. I was ready
to undertake this mission, for I could not endure the
thought that my little son might some day suffer as I
have done," continued Hanani. "And in a country
where for generations the Arabs have roved, what
security is there for any one who lives in a city without
walls?"

As Hanani said this, he looked up at the huge walls
that rose three hundred feet high around the citadel
of Susa.

"What safety, indeed?" echoed Nehe, following
his glance. "Rich and powerful as Longimanus is,
and strong as are his great armies, I would scarcely
dare live in the palace itself were it not for the walls."

"Yet I noticed that the walls of the city itself are
broken in many places," Hanani said.

"True," Nehe answered; "for since this fortress
was strengthened by Artaxerxes he has not kept
Susa's walls in repair. Who among the nations," he
continued proudly, "would venture to attack the
most powerful one on earth? And even if such a miracle should come to pass, there is room within the
citadel's gates for all the city."

"Is the palace as large as that?" Hanani asked.

"Twenty thousand men are fed at the king's table
every day of the year," Nehe answered; "and there

is room for many times that number within the palace gates. But tell me, what became of that great multitude of Jews who returned to Jerusalem some years ago to rebuild the city? It was a great feast day here, the day they set out with bands and music, and great rejoicing, to restore the city of our fathers."

"And so it was in Jerusalem when they arrived," Hanani answered, "and for a time the work went gloriously on; but it came to an end in this wise: Sanballat was a great friend of the Persian governor of our country, but he had married his daughter to the Levite, Noah."

"But," cried Nehe, "it is not lawful for a Jew to marry a woman of another nation."

"True," Hanani answered; "and when Ezra, the leader of the returned Jews, discovered Noah's heathen wife, he made Noah send her back to Sanballat, her father. Then, in revenge, Sanballat hatched this wicked plot against us. He went to the Persian governor, Rehum, and told him the Jews were but rebuilding their city in order to rebel against Longimanus, our Persian king. Rehum immediately sent this word to the king, and of course the work was stopped at once; and since then our city has lain at the mercy of any who are strong enough to attack a few thousand undefended citizens."

"It is grievous, indeed," said Nehe, sighing; "and had I not so fine a position here, I would feel as if I ought to go to Jerusalem and help to defend it from its enemies."

"My brother," cried Hanani, earnestly, "who knows but you are called to this high place in the kingdom in order to use your influence with the king, just as Esther did. Think how she helped her people when they would have been destroyed! And so may you, if you will, for surely if our city is not soon rebuilt, the Jews will all be destroyed."

The two men had been slowly walking toward the palace as they talked, and now they had reached the magnificent gateway that led to the inner walls. Before entering it Nehe pointed to a huge black shadowy building, saying:—

"This is the citadel, and there is much in it to interest you besides its armaments. In its library you will find a history of its kings that goes back for centuries, but it's written on bricks you could not read."

"It must be very interesting to you," Hanani commented.

"I have never read it," Nehe answered. "The only ancient kings who ever lived here that interested me were Hammurabi, whose code of laws the civilized world heeds more and more; and Chedorlaomer, of whom Moses wrote in our book of Genesis."

"Yes, I remember him well," Hanani said. "He joined his forces with three other kings and had a great battle with five kings in the vale of Siddim."

"Just so," Nehe smiled. "You know history well, my brother, and it may interest you to hear there is a vase in one of our temples bearing an inscription that it was taken from a temple on this expedition, and re-dedicated to the god of the conquerors."

"I'd love to see it," Hanani replied.

Hanani paused for a moment to look at the gateway in wonder. It was ninety feet high and of stone, and about twenty-five feet wide. On each side three winged bulls gazed at him from beside the gate, and as they towered nineteen feet above them, Hanani trembled, they looked so huge and terrible in the moonlight, fit emblems of the king they guarded.

"It was just outside this gate that Haman set up the gallows on which he intended to hang Mordecai," Nehe said, looking up at the gate. "You have doubtless heard the tale."

"Oh, yes," Hanani assented; "it was a favorite story with the Jews after their return to Jerusalem.

"Yes," Nehe commented. "A brave deed. None know better than those who wait upon the king how dangerous an errand it is for one to seek his presence unasked, but these are many."

As they talked, the brothers passed through the gate, and found themselves in a huge marble court which was built on a high platform. Indeed, the entire palace, with its upper gardens, rested on this platform, which was partly natural rock and partly built of brick. The palace consisted of a number of buildings, but in spite of the glorious moonlight, so dense was the shade the larger structures cast over the smaller, that to the bewildered eyes of Hanani the whole seemed one magnificent building, made up of a wilderness of marble stairways, columns, roofs, and porticoes.

He slipped his hand in the arm of Nehe, and walked close beside him. The scene was all so new and strange, a feeling half of fear and half of shyness came over Hanani, and he was very thankful he had this handsome, stately young courtier to walk beside him.

"These are the barracks of the guards," Nehe said, as they crossed the portico of a long, low building standing just inside the gate, that was swarming with men. Many of these were lounging about the entrance to their quarters, clad only in a short scarlet tunic that passed over the left shoulder, leaving the right shoulder and the right arm bare, and then fell halfway to the knee. A girdle fastened it at the waist, and held in place a short, straight sword, which seemed made rather for stabbing than for cutting. The sword was carried in a sheath, and this sheath was made more secure by being attached to the right thigh by a leather thong.

Glancing in at the open door of the soldiers' barracks as he passed, Hanani saw by the light of the torches that were held by attendants, many officers just returned from outside duty, whose coats of mail were being unlaced by their body-servants. One officer was so completely covered by his glittering armor that he looked like a huge silver fish. In one corner of the court, into which the gate led, some slingers were practising their art, the bright moonlight showing their mark almost as plainly as if it were day.

Seated in another corner an old man was telling a story to a group of soldiers lounging around him. They had made comfortable chairs for themselves by planting their huge shields of wicker work on the ground, and were leaning back against them.

"This is one of our most famous story-tellers," Nehe said, stopping before the group. "What tale are you telling to-night, Hassan?"

The old man raised his head, and when he and the men about him saw who addressed him, they all bowed themselves to the ground.

"Rise," Nehe said, "and rest you, my men. Go on with your tale, Hassan. We, too, would hear it."

"The tale I was about to tell, my lord," Hassan said, seating himself, "was of the loyalty of those Persians who followed the great Xerxes. As that king was returning on a Phœnician ship from his expedition against the Greeks, a terrible storm arose. For a time it seemed as if the waves must overwhelm and sink the vessel, but at the height of the peril Xerxes cried to the helmsman, 'Is there no escape from this danger?' 'None,' shouted the helmsman, 'unless the ship be lightened from this large body of men that crowd it. They sink it into the angry waves.' 'Then,' cried Xerxes, turning to the soldiers, 'men of Persia, now is the time for you to show your devotion to your king. My safety depends on your love.' The Persians heard him in silence, then, bowing low before him, they shouted, 'Long live King Xerxes!' and flung themselves headlong into the boiling waves, while the ship, lightened of her burden, rode safely on. Thus, O soldiers, have loyal Persians ever acted when the choice lay between their own safety and that of their king."

"Your tale is well told, Hassan," Nehe commented, as he placed a small coin in his hand. Then, turning to Hanani, he said, "Come, my brother, we must hasten on, for Bani will have finished his evening meal, and will be wondering what has become of his father."

"And all time seems long between me and my mother, but what building is this?" Hanani questioned, as they began to ascend a marble staircase.

"It is the king's own house," Nehe replied, "but his hall of audience lies there beyond." And he pointed to an edifice so enormous that its outlines were lost in the moonlight.

They walked up the staircase to a marble portico, and then past guard-rooms, where long lines of guards were stationed, and paused at a great wooden door. At the sight of the seal that dangled from Nehe's wrist, the soldiers who were guarding it lowered their long spears and gave a signal that was answered from within. The door swung open, and Hanani realized that he was in the palace of the greatest king on earth, Artaxerxes Longimanus.

CHAPTER III

COMING out of the night, for a moment Hanani's eyes were blinded by the blaze of color, and his ears were deafened by the crash of music and the voices of the men inside. Then, as his vision grew clearer, he saw that he was in a corridor paved with white and colored marbles. The vista through open golden doors showed other corridors, with pillars of polished whiteness shining out from a sea of color. Figures of marble and bronze ran along the wall, rank above rank, bathed in mysterious tints, sometimes half hidden by curtains of exquisite tints. Turn as he would, he saw those glowing colors. Soldiers and officers' slaves, bearing golden dishes heaped with fruit, magnificently clothed court officials and attendants of all grades were hurrying to and fro, and Hanani noticed that although many curious glances were cast upon him, he was not molested in any way. Everywhere heads were bent before Nehe in courteous and respectful recognition.

Passing along the corridor, Nehe led Hanani into a large hall, the golden ceiling of which was upheld by thirty-six lofty pillars, overlaid with the same precious metal. The walls were hung with silken stuff richly embroidered, and on the floor were laid softly tinted Oriental rugs. Distributed throughout the room were beautiful tables at which guests were reclining on luxurious couches, and they were served by bare-footed slaves, black as night, whose arms and necks were loaded with bracelets and chains of gold.

"Is the king here?" Hanani asked, glancing around at the tables.

"Oh, no," Nehe answered; "Artaxerxes always dines alone, save at the great feast, once a year, or when he is with Queen Damaspia in her private apartments. But come, let us hasten to my own chamber, where we can talk unheard."

Then, crossing the room, he led the way to another corridor similar to the first, and presently paused before a tall narrow doorway, the wooden door of which, opening inward, was closed and fastened by bars and an enormous lock. The entrance was guarded by six eunuchs. They were the first Hanani had ever seen, and when Nehe called his attention to them he turned and regarded them curiously.

They had the same general appearance — low foreheads, small round noses, full lips, bloated cheeks, and large double chins. They were dressed, too, in a fashion peculiar to themselves. Instead of the short tunic of leather, silk, linen, or mail that the other guards wore, their long, narrow gowns, fringed at the edge, came almost to their feet, and had tight, short sleeves. They wore earrings and glittering armlets and bracelets. In spite of the splendor of their dress, Hanani turned away shuddering from the cruel, cunning glitter of their sharp, bright, questioning eyes.

"This is the entrance to the harem," Nehe said; "and our mother's apartments are here. She is as high in the favor of the queen as I am in that of the king. Jewesses have found favor in the court since Queen Esther's day."

Hanani turned impulsively toward the bull-guarded gateway.

"Oh, let us enter!" he said. "My very heart cries out for a sight of my mother."

Nehe caught him by the arm.

"My brother," he exclaimed, "if your foot had but crossed that portal, not all the influence in the kingdom would have saved your life! It is the king's right and that of the eunuchs alone, to enter there. Come, let us hasten away! Already those guards gaze at us much too steadily. I will send word to my mother, and she will come to us, and you shall see her in due season. Here is my own room, where you shall find safety and rest."

Nehe paused before a doorway draped with a silken curtain, and, drawing it aside, led the way into a magnificent apartment, saying as he did so:—

"Welcome, my brother! Peace be with you!"

Hanani had expected a beautiful room, but the one into which he was ushered was so magnificent that he paused on the threshold, overcome for a moment with surprise.

The apartment was long and narrow, and the floor was covered with a rich Persian carpet, whose texture and tints were so exquisite, Hanani hesitated to place his foot upon it, although in obedience to the Eastern custom, his sandals had already been removed and his feet bathed in a beautiful bronze basin by a slave who had knelt at the door of the banquet hall.

Silver lamps hung by silver chains from the ceiling, and richly carved stools and very high tables were scattered around the apartment.

On one of these tables rested a jewelled cup on a golden tray.

So exquisite was its workmanship that Hanani involuntarily went forward to examine it. As he put out his hand, however, a soldier who was standing by the table quickly drew his short sword from his girdle, and interposed it between Hanani's hand and the treasured cup.

Hanani drew back with a start.

"It seemeth me the king's palace is a dangerous place for a poor Hebrew, my brother," he said.

Nehe smiled as he answered:—

"You can hardly expect to touch the king's cup, my brother. I am his cup-bearer, and my life is the forfeit if harm come to the king through the cup. A drop of poison in this cup, my Hanani, and Persia lacks a king and you lack a brother. Hence my most trustworthy soldiers guard it day and night. Arbaces, let me take it. I would show it to my brother."

The soldier sheathed his sword, and Nehe lifted the precious vessel and held it under the lamp, that Hanani might examine it.

The base of the cup was a beautifully modelled lion's head, from which the cup itself arose, shaped like a lily, and studded with precious stones. In spite of its beauty, as it lay sparkling in Nehe's hand, Hanani was glad when he restored it to its place on the gold tray, and as he did so an overwhelming sense of his brother's responsibility as cup-bearer to the king swept over Hanani.

"I thought Jerusalem without walls a dangerous place," he said, "but methinks, brother, that when one considers the enemies a king like Longimanus must have, it is as safe as this great walled city. A drop of poison is as dangerous to a king as an army to a city. I wonder not you guard your cup, or that the king must greatly trust his cup-bearer."

As he spoke a shrill cry of "Oh, father, my father!" attracted Hanani's attention, and looking down the apartment, he saw his little son endeavoring to climb down from a high stool that stood by one of the tables.

"Wait, Bani," called Nehe, cheerily; "let us come to you, little man. Have you left us some honey and grapes?"

The little fellow smiled contentedly, and the two hastened to him. As his father took the seat Nehe designated, he said sadly: —

"Oh, Bani, what would I not give if only your mother and brother were here to-night!" And he glanced at the table laden with fruit and meat and milk, and then bowed his head, as was the custom of the Hebrews, turning his face toward Jerusalem, and praying for the protection of the Lord God over his dear ones.

When he raised it again, Nehe said: —

"And now, brother, I will see if I can get speech with our mother to-night. I long to see her joy when she knows you are really alive."

So saying, he turned to one of his attendants and ordered: —

"Give me my writing materials."

The man bowed low, and a moment later placed before Nehe a small roll of papyrus, on which the cupbearer hastily wrote a few words in the Hebrew characters; and then, sealing it with his seal, he ordered the man to carry it to the eunuch Eros, asking him if possible to give it at once to the Lady Sarai.

"None of the inmates of the harem are allowed to leave its doors," Nehe resumed, turning to Hanani, "save when they follow the king. But my mother once saved the young queen's life, and as she is a Hebrew, the king allows her, and her own maidens not in the harem, to visit my apartments. So I hope to see her soon. And now let us eat and refresh ourselves, and you shall tell me what I can do to help you."

"But first," cried Hanani, lifting his goblet of sparkling water, "tell me of yourself, for I know nothing of you since you were stolen away, scarce more than a baby, sobbing in my mother's arms."

"I have no memory of that terrible scene," mused Nehe, "but my mother has told me that we were carried to the handsome city of Samaria. Here we

were seen by a Persian general, who was so struck
with the beauty of my father and mother that he
bought us for a present to King Artaxerxes. The
king soon took my father into his service as a gardener, and my mother was sent to wait on the queen
dowager. Her skill as a needlewoman earned the
queen's favor, and she gradually rose until she became head lady to the present queen. She is now the
most trusted of her Majesty's attendants. My
father's rare skill as a gardener stood him, too, in
good stead, for the Persian nobles, while they despise
and scorn trade of all kinds, holding that it teaches
men to lie, consider gardening an honorable occupa-
tion. He was soon appointed chief gardener to the
king — a position of great honor and importance, in
which he heaped up large riches."

"Then he had many years in which to enjoy his
honors and wealth," Hanani commented.

"Yes; he lived until a year ago," Nehe answered,
"and then died full of years and honors."

"Did you live with him all that time?"

"No," Nehe replied, taking a bunch of luscious
grapes from a golden tray that a kneeling slave held
up to him; "I was left with my parents until I was
five years old. Then the king's chamberlain, seeing I
was a sturdy little fellow, entered me in the royal

school, and there I remained until I was fifteen, when
I became a member of the king's bodyguard, though
my training in the school still continued."

"What were you taught?"

"We learned all the ceremonies of the court, and
were taught to hunt, to ride, to shoot with the bow,
to handle the sword, and, above all else, to speak the
truth. Indeed, to be a page in the king's school was
no light matter. Long before daylight the awakeners
went from room to room, calling the boys. How we
hated their 'Rise you, rise you, my masters!' But we
hated still more the touch of their long black whips,
and so, no matter how dark it was, or cold and chill
on a winter's morning, we quickly rose at their stern
call. Hastily dressing ourselves and drinking a glass
of milk, we went out into the marble court you saw
in front of the palace, and began our day's work.
There we were taught to run like deer and to ride as
though we were part of a horse itself. I assure you,
no Arab of the desert can sit his horse more securely
than the boys of the king's school. By the time we
were seven we could send an arrow straight to the
mark at fifty paces, and at nine we were accomplished horsemen. What gala days those were for us
when the king and his court came out into the field
and watched us as we raced at full speed before them,

throwing our javelins and shooting our arrows with unerring aim as our horses thundered by! At ten years old we began to join the court on its hunting expeditions, and it was the skill with which I ran down and killed a wild boar, that was in the act of goring a favorite dog of the king's, that first gained me the monarch's favor, a favor that he has not withdrawn from that day to this.

"We lived on the plainest fare, and many days we went hungry, for part of our training was to teach us to seek food for ourselves when we were in the forest. So we grew up strong, sturdy, honest youths, fit material for the warlike nation of the Persians."

"How strange it all is," said Hanani, "that we two brothers should have had such a different youth."

"I don't think it was so very different, brother," Nehe replied. "You learned to ride and shoot, to till the ground and tell the truth, and so did I; and as for danger, perchance the inmate of the palace is not more safe than he who dwells in the field. But I think our mother approaches."

CHAPTER IV

AS Nehe spoke, the silken curtains were drawn aside from the doorway, and the attendant announced: —

"My Lord Nehe, your mother, the Lady Sarai, awaits your pleasure."

Both the brothers arose, but a gesture from Nehe restrained Hanani from advancing, while he himself went forward.

As Nehe did so, Hanani's eyes were riveted on the lady who now entered the room. She was only a little past fifty, and her majestic figure was as upright as a girl's. Her wavy black hair was smoothed back to her ears, and then held in place by a fillet of gold set with pearls. A long robe of white silk, with a heavy gold fringe, fell to her ankles, and her small and well-formed feet were shod with delicate sandals.

The lady's beautiful arms were bare, but were partly concealed by a short cloak of violet silk, richly embroidered and fringed, which fell to her waist. Her face was sweet and attractive. The sensitive mouth drooped at the corners, as do the mouths of those that have suffered, and her large, brilliant, dark eyes had a pathetic look; but they were eyes that could smile as well as weep, and the whole face was one that showed a sweet, pure, strong nature.

A slender girlish figure walked beside her, dressed entirely in white. Her face was concealed by the veil that fell over it, but her arms, bare to the shoulder, gleamed through the mist of her veil in shapely beauty. According to the Persian custom, she held in her hand a crimson rose.

As Sarai and her maiden stepped inside the doorway, a eunuch followed her, and stood with folded hands awaiting her pleasure. Apparently oblivious to all around him, the eunuch's keen, searching eyes took in every detail of the little group before him, and his ears were strained to catch the faintest whisper. Every soldier and attendant in the room looked askance at him as he stood there, for they realized that here was one of the spies of the harem. Here was the means by which the cruel queen mother kept herself informed of all that went on within the walls of the palace, and many a noble's life had hung on the word of this heavy-browed man, standing there seemingly as silent and as motionless as a statue.

The Lady Sarai came forward eagerly to meet Nehe, holding out both hands and exclaiming: —

"My son, naught has gone amiss, I hope? Your note alarmed me, bidding my speedy attendance here; but one look at your face tells me all is well."

"Yes, mother," Nehe answered; "but since the time I saw you faint when news of father's safe return from battle was given you, I have feared almost as much to give you good news as to give you bad."

"And what good news have you for me, Nehe?" she asked, taking his hand and kissing him on both cheeks. "You are well and prosperous. That is all that can give me pleasure now."

"Mother," Nehe said tenderly, as he gazed into her sweet, dark eyes, "mother, tell me, truly, what was the saddest hour you ever knew?"

The Lady Sarai's lips quivered as she replied: —

"My son, you doubtless think I shall answer, the hour your father died; but no. Hachaliah went to his death at a good old age. He was many years older than I, and, captive though he was, he had all the comfort that love could give him; but, oh, Nehe!"

"Yes, mother," the young man said tenderly.

"Oh, Nehe, you do not remember Hanani, your brother, my sturdy, beautiful boy, and whom I hid in the flax and left dying, the day we were carried captive. Oh, Hanani, my boy, my boy!" she cried passionately, "how his feeble little hands strove to hold me, as I drew the flax over him, and though his eyes were fast closing in unconsciousness, how wistfully they looked at me, as he moaned, 'Mother, mother! do not leave me!' Sometimes I wake in the night and hear that cry ringing in my ears. Nehe, all these years my empty arms have ached for my firstborn, my Hanani! The hour I left him — that was the saddest, the very saddest hour of all my life. But why do you speak of it to-night, dear son?" And Lady Sarai looked inquiringly at Nehe, as her maiden, who had drawn close to her, laid one hand caressingly on her arm, in deepest sympathy.

"Because, mother," Nehe replied earnestly, "did you ever think that, perhaps Hanani might not have died?"

"Only to pray that he did," the Lady Sarai answered. "How could the child live on alone in that country, desolated in turn by the Arab and Egyptian? And yet never a night since then has passed that I have not prayed, 'Lord God of my fathers, if he lives, preserve him in peace, and in the religion of his fathers!' It breaks my heart to think my son may be a worshipper of Bel."

"And God heard your prayer, mother," exclaimed Hanani, no longer able to restrain himself. And, springing forward, he fell on his knees before the beautiful woman, catching her hands in his, and covering them with his tears and kisses.

She gave a cry of utter astonishment, and then her eyes fairly devoured the handsome, expressive face of the man before her. For a moment incredulity and astonishment dominated her; then a look of intense tenderness and happiness grew in her eyes. Bending forward she threw her arms around Hanani, drawing him close to her, and exclaiming: —

"Hanani, my son! my son!"

Meantime little Bani had followed his father across the long apartment, and now he seized hold of Lady Sarai's gown, crying: —

"Pretty lady, Bani kiss 'oo, too."

And Sarai, looking down, saw what seemed to her bewildered eyes the face of the child she had left dying in Judea more than twenty years before. The same hair, blue eyes, and thin, expressive lips of his father looked up at her. This face, however, bloomed in health and beauty, and that had been thin and pale with disease.

"Hanani!" she cried, sobbing and catching him in her arms. "Oh, how I have searched every boyish face all these years for just a chance look of you, and now at last here you are! Is it a miracle?" she asked. "Has God sent me two sons in place of one?"

"No, no, mother," Nehe answered, laughing for very joy in her delight, "but you have a son restored, and a grandson. Come, let us sit down, and you shall hear all the strange, yea, wonderful things that Hanani has to tell. It may be," he added, "that God has sent us first to this far country, and kept Hanani there in Palestine, that our hearts might be moved to save others from suffering as you have done."

So saying, Nehe led his mother to a luxurious chair, which she took, though she still kept Bani clasped in her arms while her eyes scarcely left Hanani's face for an instant.

It was some time before Hanani could take up the history of his life, for Lady Sarai interrupted him constantly with caresses and questions; but at last it was all told, — of the servant's faithful care, of Hanani's marriage to Hannah, of the breaking up of his home, and at last of how his wife and child were even now prisoners of the cruel and treacherous Sanballat, and how Hanani had come to Susa, hoping he might obtain an audience with King Longimanus, and plead the cause of the defenceless Jews in the unwalled city of Jerusalem.

Long and earnestly they talked, and many were the plans suggested and set aside each time with the significant words, "Too dangerous."

"Why?" Hanani asked at last, "why do you constantly say 'too dangerous,' mother? Is it not safe for a subject to see his king?"

"My son," the Lady Sarai answered, "when you think of a king, you think of such a one as Solomon was, or David, but you must know, Hanani, that a Persian king is in the eyes of his people a god. None may enter his presence unsummoned, on pain of death, — not even the queen; and if a complaint were made concerning the defenceless city, he might think, indeed he would be almost sure to take it for granted, that you were planning an insurrection, and then he would order your instant death. And such a death, to be buried alive or crucified! These are two of the least painful of the many forms of Persian punishment! No, no! it is not to be thought of! We will wait, my Hanani, and we will take counsel with the wisest of our people. We will pray, and the God of our fathers will suggest to us some plea that we may make that will turn the king's heart to us, and yet not endanger more than need be the one who makes it. And now I must go."

The two young men arose as the Lady Sarai did, and Hanani turned toward his mother and said earnestly: —

"I did not realize the difficulty of the task that lay

before me, mother. Yes, yes, we must pray that God will show us the way."

Nehe held out his hand, and as his mother moved little Bani to her other arm in order to take it, the child awakened.

"Give him to me, mother," Hanani said. "He is my little man now." And he stood the boy gently on the floor.

The child looked toward the huge eunuch, who was still standing inside the doorway, where the Lady Sarai had left him, and, attracted by his golden earrings and bracelets, moved toward him.

Nehe turned around. "Adna!" he said, and then, laying his hand on his mother's arm, he smiled and pointed across the room. The Lady Sarai's glance followed his, and then she, too, smiled, and a sweet, merry look came over her face as she called: —

"Lydia, I need your attendance to replace my veil."

Hanani, struck by her tone of merry raillery, turned quickly also, and the picture that caught his eye was certainly pretty enough to hold the laughing gaze of all three. No wonder Sarai's voice was soft as music in spite of its laughing note, as she called, "Lydia!" for Nehe's handsome armor-bearer, Adna, clad in his yellow silk tunic, was bending eagerly

over Lydia, their graceful forms outlined against the
crimson tapestry of the wall. Lydia, taking advantage of the absorption of her mistress, had drawn
aside her veil, as was the custom in the apartments
of the Jews, and had retreated to the shadow of a
tall pillar in one corner of the room. Here Adna,
fancying himself unnoticed, followed her, and the
little group of two had been as deeply absorbed in a
low conversation, at that side of the room, as had
been the larger group at the other.

Apparently Adna had been pleading earnestly with
the lovely girl for some favor, for at last she raised
the crimson rose, and, dropping her beautiful eyes,
while a bright smile dimpled over her face, handed it
to him, saying softly: —

"Take it, then. 'Tis but a rose."

The youth took it, answering earnestly: —

"But it has lain in your hand," and raised it to his
lips.

Unluckily for Adna, it was just at this moment
that Nehe, needing his services, sent a searching
glance around the room, and discovered his retreat.
Both young people started as Sarai called, and the
rose Adna held was scarcely as red as the fair cheeks
of Lydia as she hastily dropped her veil over them,
and came timidly forward to do her mistress's bid-

ding. But Adna came toward them with head erect
and shining eyes, thrusting the rose into his tunic,
looking as one who has been honored by a king and
gained a princely boon.

As Lydia adjusted her mistress's veil, Nehe turned
to Lady Sarai and said: —

"Mother, I wish you would not bring that eunuch
Barras when you come to my chamber. He hates me,
because I know him too well. I fear he will do me
some harm."

The Lady Sarai looked startled.

"What harm could he do you, Nehe?" she asked.

"I know not, my mother," Nehe answered, "but
I like not the look in his evil eyes. To-night, as we
have talked, he has been glancing around and
around the apartment. I am sure the man means
harm."

As Nehe spoke, there was a sudden flash at the end
of the room. The silver chain which held one of the
lamps gave way, and the lamp was dashed to the
floor, just at the side of the silken curtains. In an
instant they caught fire, and the flame leaped up the
doorway, reaching out red arms to the linen draperies
that hung on either side. Every one sprang forward
to put out the fire, and for a few moments all was
confusion and terror. But the blaze proved a slight

one, for the flames were extinguished almost as quickly as they had caught, and Nehe congratulated himself that no more damage had been done than the loss of a few curtains.

The servants were busy removing the burnt finery, when the soldier who guarded the king's cup quickly approached Nehe, saying excitedly: —

"My lord, the cup! The king's cup is gone!"

"It cannot be far," Nehe replied. "It has been knocked from the table in the confusion. Arbaces," he added reproachfully, "why did you not guard it?"

"My lord," Arbaces replied respectfully, "in the confusion of the fire some one knocked against me, and I tripped and fell. When I recovered myself, the cup was gone!"

They all turned and walked to the table where the cup had stood, and began a rapid search for it on the floor and beneath the furniture. Scarcely had they done so, when Barras came forward with a deep obeisance.

"My lord," he said, handing Nehe the precious vessel, "it would not please the king were he to know that I found his cup rolling in a corner of your room."

Nehe flushed hotly.

"Had you not been here, perhaps it would not have been found there," he said significantly.

The eunuch's dark eyes flashed, but he said nothing, and the Lady Sarai interposed sweetly: —

"Never mind, Nehe! The cup has been found. No harm has been done. Good night!"

Then, kissing her sons, she bestowed a farewell caress on little Bani, and left the apartment, followed by the eunuch and Lydia. As she did so, Nehe set the cup back in its place on the table, regarding it closely.

"I like not the look of that eunuch," he said; "but I am glad the cup is safe."

CHAPTER V

THE torches were being extinguished in the harem when Lady Sarai entered its corridor, and, after stopping for a whispered word with the eunuch who guarded the queen's apartment, she passed on to her own room. Barras respectfully drew aside the curtain for her to enter, and then retraced his steps to the door of the queen's apartment.

"Eros," he said vehemently, to the guard, "a word with the queen! a word with the queen! It is a matter of life or death to the king!"

"Wait, then, and you shall see her!" Eros replied, and hastily entered her room.

A moment after he reappeared, saying:—

"Enter! the queen will see you!"

Drawing aside the silken curtains which hid the doorway, Eros ushered Barras into the presence of Queen Damaspia, who was reclining on a magnificent couch, covered with a robe of white silk, embroidered with pearls. Above the couch climbed the golden vine which had been given to her husband's grandfather, the great Darius, by Pythias the Lydian. The queen lay in the shadow of the canopy which the vine upheld, but as Barras approached the couch, it seemed to him that each priceless jewel in the clusters that hung there was a piercing eye gazing into his guilty soul.

A maiden kneeling near her mistress's head was softly strumming on a harp an accompaniment to a low, sweet slumber song. At a gesture from her mistress she hushed her notes, and, as the eunuch prostrated himself, the queen said haughtily: —

"Rise, Barras! and tell me what brings you here at this late hour. Your errand must be one of life or death, indeed, to make you risk my displeasure by disturbing me when I have sought repose."

Barras arose and stood with his hands folded submissively before his royal mistress.

"My errand, indeed, is one of life or death," he answered meekly; "the life, my queen, of thy husband, King Artaxerxes Longimanus."

"What mean you?" cried the queen, springing to her feet. "Is there a plot among the eunuchs to murder him, as his father, the great Xerxes, was murdered?"

"Nay, nay," Barras answered hastily; "there is no danger to-night, lady queen. It will come to-morrow, and by the hand of his cup-bearer, Nehe the Jew. I was in attendance upon Lady Sarai to his apartments to-night, and overheard the plot. Lord Nehe would create dissensions here in the kingdom, and then flee back to his own country and establish him himself there as king."

"Nehe, the king's favorite, and Sarai, my most trusted attendant!" exclaimed the queen, white with horror. "Send for her instantly."

The kneeling girl sprang to her feet and quitted the room. A moment later she returned, followed by Sarai and Lydia.

"Now," said the queen, turning to the eunuch, "tell again the story you have just begun."

The eunuch's cruel eyes fell before the frightened, searching gaze that Lady Sarai bent on him, but he began his tale glibly enough: —

"I attended, this evening, my Lady Sarai to the apartments of her son, the Lord Nehe, cup-bearer to our gracious king. She went there to meet a son who had just come from Jerusalem, and who detailed to her and my Lord Nehe a plot to rebuild the walls of the city and establish the cup-bearer as ruler. Knowing King Artaxerxes would never give his consent to have his favorite leave him, they spoke in low tones of some plan to rid themselves of the king. I could not catch their words, but several times I saw them glance toward the king's cup, and as we were leaving, my brother, who is in attendance on Lord Nehe, whispered to me: —

"'Warn the queen! The cup is poisoned, and Nehe attends the king to-morrow!'

"'Are you sure?' I asked.

"'Quite sure,' he answered. 'If the queen would have proof, let her send hither and examine the cup.'

"And now, lady queen, let a messenger be sent for the king's physician, and let the cup be examined."

"It is well said," answered the queen. "Barras, do you go at once for the king's physician, and the cup shall be sent for as well."

"But to obtain that," Eros said, respectfully interrupting, "a permit must be had from the king himself, and the chamberlain will have to get that for me."

"Let Barras then go for the physician," the queen said eagerly, "and go yourself to the chamberlain. The matter must be investigated quietly and quickly. Say no more than need be to the king to-night. Nehe was my playfellow when I was a child, and he has rendered me many a service since he has been cup-bearer. I would not see him lose his life to-night, if this charge be not true, but alas! I greatly fear it is."

Barras, his face lighted with an evil smile, hurriedly

departed on his errand, while the Lady Sarai sank, half fainting, to the floor. She knew how lightly the king and queen held the lives of their subjects, that even a suspicion was enough to send a man to the torture chamber; and she realized, if poison were found in the cup, that her son would be allowed no defence. Then she recalled the events of the evening. She remembered Nehe's expressed fear of Barras, and a thrill of terror ran through her as she thought of the missing cup, and how it had been found by the eunuch.

"Alas!" she sobbed to herself, "he must have poisoned it then. Oh, Nehe! my son, my son!"

The voice of the queen aroused her, its usually kind notes made cold and bitter by the deadly suspicion that had entered Damaspia's heart.

"Is it true," she was saying, "you spent this evening in your son's room, discussing a plan to rebuild Jerusalem?"

"It is true, O my queen," Sarai answered, lifting her white face hopelessly. "True, we discussed a plan to rebuild Jerusalem, but with the king's consent."

"Damaspia, my queen!" suddenly cried Lydia, throwing herself on her knees beside the Lady Sarai, "you may send me to the torture chamber if it be

your wish, but I will tell the truth. I was with my
lady, and heard the words that Lord Nehe spoke of
his own city, and of King Artaxerxes, and they were
words of kindness, O my queen! They were not words
of treachery and death."

"Hush, maid!" the queen said sternly. "This is no
question for you to discuss. We shall know when the
cup comes if it be poisoned or not. Here is my messenger now."

As she said this, Barras entered, and, prostrating
himself, told her that the king's physician was not in
his room, and his servants knew not where he was,
but he would return in an hour, and when he came,
he would be instantly brought to the queen.

"Only an hour!" the Lady Sarai repeated to herself, and a wild thought ran through her head of sending a warning to her son; but it was instantly dismissed. Every motion she made was now watched by
a hundred eager eyes, and already her attitude of
utter dejection was commented on. As she thought
of this she sprang to her feet.

"Queen Damaspia," she cried, "Nehe is innocent!
Barras has poisoned the cup! But God, the God of
the Israelites, will save my son! He is innocent!
Human aid I may not give him, but to my God I will
pray."

Then, kneeling down on the marble floor, she turned her face toward Jerusalem, and betook herself to prayer, while Lydia, standing close at her side with uplifted face and folded hands, showed that she, too, joined in her mistress's petition.

CHAPTER VI

SCARCELY had the curtains of Nehe's apartment been drawn behind the Lady Sarai and her attendants, when Hanani stooped to pick up little Bani, saying as he did so: —

"It is time this small fellow was at rest. He has had a hard day."

As he raised the child in his arms, he saw he was deadly pale, and his face was drawn with a look of terrible pain.

"Bani sick," the child said. "Ze nasty stuff in ze pitty cup made Bani sick," he explained.

Nehe uttered an exclamation of horror.

"What do you mean?" he cried. "Oh, Hanani, I fear the child is poisoned."

"Ze naughty cup, ze cup," the child reiterated, and then his blue eyes closed and he sank unconscious into the arms of his father.

"He is dead," Hanani cried; "oh, Nehe, the child is dead?"

"No, no, my brother," Nehe answered; "not as yet."

Then, turning to one of the many attendants who were crowding around, he cried: —

"Run, Adna, run, give this seal to Ramon, the physician of the king, and bring him here at once."

In a very few minutes the curtains were again drawn aside, and the great Ramon hurried in.

"I met your messenger in the hall," he said, "and hastened here, my lord, at your bidding."

In a moment more he was bending over the dying Bani.

"The child has been poisoned," Ramon said at last, looking up from Bani into the anxious faces bending over him. "Have you any idea what did it?"

"None," replied Nehe. "He said 'ze pretty cup' made him sick, but we do not know what cup."

"Pretty cup," repeated Ramon, the physician, glancing around the room. Nehe's eyes followed his. Suddenly they rested on the king's golden cup.

"Arbaces," he cried, "has Bani touched the cup?"

"My lord," answered the frightened soldier, flinging himself at Nehe's feet, "alas! after Barras set the cup on the table, Bani stood by it. One hand held yours as you talked with the Lady Sarai, and the other — "

"The other?" Nehe questioned sternly, as Arbaces paused.

"With the other," the soldier faltered, "the child touched the inside of the cup, and then I saw him put his finger in his mouth and suck his finger, as if it were something he liked. Barras the eunuch saw it, too, and he plucked the child's arm from the back, but oh, my lord, I dreamed of no harm to the cup or the child, and I liked not to disturb your conversation."

Nehe's face fairly blazed in his horror and indignation.

"The cup has been poisoned!" he cried. "Barras did it while we were searching for it. Here, O Ramon, see if you can find the species of poison it contains!"

The physician laid Bani in his father's arms and took the cup, while all the group gathered around him, peering anxiously into its shining depth.

"Do you clean the king's cup with oil, my Lord Nehe?" he asked at length.

"With oil, my Lord Ramon?" Nehe faltered. "No, no; with water; only the purest water, such as is brought for the king's own use in silver flagons from the clear stream of the Choaspes."

"And yet," said the physician, drawing the end of the fine linen scarf that encircled his waist carefully over the inner surface of the cup, "and yet here is oil! Poisoned oil has been carefully rubbed on it, and the child has received part of the dose intended for the king. It is the poison well known to all the eunuchs of the palace. More than once have I met it; mostly in the mouths of dead men," he added grimly.

"And he will die!" cried Hanani, in an agonized tone, gazing into the pallid face of his boy.

"No," answered the physician. "Poisons have antidotes. The quantity he received was very small. We will give him this, and he will soon revive."

So saying, he took a small alabaster box from a slave who attended him, and poured a few drops of the brown liquid it contained down the throat of the unconscious child.

"There," he exclaimed, a few minutes later, as Bani sighed deeply and then opened his blue eyes, "had the physician of the great Darius known of this powerful elixir, Darius had not died. And you, my fine fellow, will live to give your father many another anxious moment, I dare say."

Nehe clasped Hanani's hand in an ecstasy of happiness.

"Rejoice, my brother," he cried. "Bani is saved, thanks to the good physician." And both brothers turned to Ramon and poured out their heartfelt gratitude.

The physician listened to them a moment in silence, and then he said: —

"My Lord Nehe, suspicion is a terrible thing. He who put poison in yon cup will not wait long to damage you."

Nehe started, and then seized the vessel.

"Run," he said, turning to one of the slaves; "fetch me hot water and linen cloths. All trace of the poison must be removed at once! And listen, as you value your lives! Mention not to any one what has happened here this night."

The slave soon returned with hot water and cloths, and Ramon added something to the water, with which Nehe immediately scoured the cup, relating to the physician as he did so his suspicion of Barras, and the cause of it.

At last the cup was cleansed to the satisfaction of Nehe, and of the physician, and, after seeing it restored to its place, Ramon moved toward the door. Just as he was about to pass through, his unshod foot trod upon a small object. Stooping, he picked up a tiny silver stopper. He held it carefully to the light and then smelled it.

"Ah," he said, "here is the top of the bottle that contained the poison. I wonder where the rest is." And he began looking about him on the floor. Nehe went forward and joined in the search, but no flagon could be found.

They were interrupted by the doorkeeper, who announced: —

"A messenger from Queen Damaspia."

And Eros, chief of the eunuchs, with two of the palace guards, stepped into the room. He bowed low before Nehe, and, handing him a seal ring, said: —

"Queen Damaspia commands my Lord Nehe to send immediately to her the king's cup."

Nehe turned pale, but, pointing to the cup, he said: —

"There it stands, Eros! I trust it to your integrity. Guard it as your life, and deliver it to the queen untouched by any hand save yours."

"I will keep it with the utmost care, my Lord Nehe," Eros answered. "I have not forgotten the kindness your mother once showed me when I lay sick of a fever." And, taking up the cup, he left the apartment.

When Eros was gone, Nehe dismissed all his attendants and paced the room with an anxious countenance.

"My life is in great danger this night, Hanani," he said. "One of two things only can save me: either that no charge be made against me, or that the one who poisoned the cup be discovered. I know it was Barras, but I cannot prove it."

"Surely," Hanani answered, "the king would not take your life on a mere suspicion. You can prove your innocence to any judge."

Nehe smiled a sad smile.

"No chance will be given to me. Yonder in the queen's apartments we know that a charge is made. If the queen deems me guilty, she will tell the king, and by morning I shall be buried alive or stoned to death by the wayside."

"Oh, my brother, my brother!" Hanani exclaimed. "can such injustice be? Let me hasten to the king and plead for you."

"It is useless," Nehe answered. "You could not see him."

"But have you no friend who would take him a message?"

"And meet almost certain death for so doing?" Nehe replied despondently. "No, Hanani, there is no appeal from the sentence of the king, nor any hope of mercy. Often, indeed, men are put to death who know not their offence. How can I hope for mercy from one who sentenced his own brother unheard?"

"Did Artaxerxes do that? It is too horrible to be true."

"It is true," Nehe answered. "All the court knew at the time that the mighty Xerxes was killed by

Artebanus and a eunuch. But Artaxerxes believed the story they told him that Darius did it, and so he had him assassinated."

"Did the king ever learn the truth?"

"Yes, to his great sorrow; but not until the traitor Artebanus had tried to murder him in his own bed-chamber. Then Artaxerxes realized how unjust he had been to his brother, and his grief was terrible. It is for the murdered prince that the heir apparent is named Darius."

"But it is too dreadful to be borne," Hanani cried, springing to his feet and pacing the apartment. "Are we to do nothing — nothing! — to save your life? Oh, Nehe, this is no place for a Hebrew! Better the unwalled city of Jerusalem, where a man may at least fight for himself, than the gilded splendor of a court where a man's life lies in the careless grasp of a cruel and irresponsible monarch."

"Perhaps," Nehe answered reverently; "but if human aid cannot reach me — the God of the Hebrews has done wonderful things in this land to save His faithful servants when danger threatened. Our nation He may have deserted, but He did not desert those who trusted Him. Many a time when I have been attending the king in Babylon have I looked down into the den of lions where Daniel was thrown.

And have you not heard of the three youths in the king's school who were cast into the furnace of fire, yet God saved them? My father used to show me the glittering image that they refused to worship, and he prayed God to give me strength to do as they did, should I ever need it."

"But," said Hanani, sadly, "you are only a courtier in the palace of a worshipper of Ormazd. Why should our God send His angels to save you this night, Nehemiah?"

"Because," exclaimed Nehe, springing to his feet also, and raising his hand reverently, "if the God of the Hebrews saves my life this night, I will devote it to His service, instead of to that of King Longimanus. If I be saved, forty days will I spend in fasting and prayer. Then I will ask of the king that I may go to the help of my people, and God Himself shall put words into my mouth that my request be not refused. All that I am, all that I have, I give my God this night."

"And your prayer shall be heard," cried Hanani; "surely, surely, your prayer shall be heard!"

CHAPTER VII

FOR an hour Lady Sarai and Lydia knelt silent and motionless in prayer, while the queen and her attendants discussed in eager and excited tones the story the eunuch had told them.

The queen was becoming very restless and impatient, when the tramp of swift feet was heard, and Sarai, looking up from her devotions, saw Eros enter, bearing the king's cup on its golden salver.

Barras stepped forward to give it to the queen. As he reached out his hand to take it, the Lady Sarai cried: —

"My queen, I pray you let no hand save yours touch the cup until the physician examines it."

"Your request is granted," the queen answered, "and here comes Ramon at last. Sir," she said, as the physician entered and prostrated himself before her, "there is the king's cup. Will you examine it and tell us if there is aught here to work harm to my lord?"

The physician took the cup and regarded it closely.

"I see nothing here that can do harm," he said presently, "but let your Majesty have it filled with wine, and I can better tell."

Wine was immediately poured into the cup, and then the physician, turning to Barras, said: —

"Drink, Barras, drink, and let me see its effect."

For answer, the eunuch fell at the queen's feet in an agony of terror, beseeching her to spare his life.

As he did so the Lady Sarai sprang forward and fell on her knees before the queen.

"Let me drink of the wine!" she cried eagerly; "I fear no cup my son sends here!"

And, lifting it, she drank its contents.

For a few minutes the eyes of all in the apartment were fixed on the Lady Sarai, and then, as no evil effects were observed, they turned on the eunuch, who crouched tremblingly on the ground.

"How dared you make so unfounded a charge against the king's favorite?" demanded the queen, angrily, looking down on him.

"Because he intended to make it come true, your Majesty," said the physician. "Let the guard search him, and proof of his guilt may be found."

In an instant the hands of the queen's guard were going through Barras's garments.

"We find nothing on him," said Eros, at last.

"Nothing?" repeated Ramon, looking scornfully at the eunuch. "What is that tangled in the fringe of his sash?"

Eros stooped and took up a small silver flagon that had evidently been secreted in the eunuch's sleeve, and which he had vainly attempted to drop.

"I thought you would find something if you looked carefully," Ramon said, examining the bottle. "This flagon contained the poison that was put into the king's cup to-night, and here," he continued, drawing the stopper from his tunic, "is its lid. You dropped this Barras, in your haste, when you broke the chain that held the lamp in place in my Lord Nehe's room to-night. See, we will fit it on!"

And Ramon screwed the stopper carefully in place.

Exclamations of horror and astonishment broke from the little group as he did so, while the eunuch muttered: —

"'Twas but a magic potion the priest gave me for a fever."

"Then drink it yourself," said Ramon, holding the flagon close to his trembling lips.

Barras took it and essayed to raise it to his mouth, and then, with a look of utter despair, sank grovelling at the queen's feet. The physician turned to Damaspia.

"Does my lady queen wish more proof as to who was willing to risk poisoning the king himself, if he could but ruin his favorite?"

"No," cried the queen, spurning the prostrate and trembling culprit with her foot. "It is enough! Die, and to-night! Die, by that worst of all deaths; die by the boat!"

A scream of horrible fear rang through the room, and two attendants stepped forward. They covered the eunuch's face, raised him from the floor, and bore him away.

CHAPTER VIII

ALL night long Nehe and Hanani knelt in prayer or talked in low, earnest tones. At last the gray light of dawn came peeping through the curtains that veiled the windows, and their suspense grew to agony.

"Let us go out upon the portico, Hanani," Nehe said desperately. "This air stifles me. I cannot breathe. I would see the sun rise even if it be the last I shall ever see, for nowhere rises the sun more gloriously than here on the plains of Persia."

The two brothers stepped out upon the expansive porch, and for a moment almost forgot the horror that hung over them in watching the beautiful scene that unfolded before their eyes. Magnificent marble stairways, the beauty of whose architecture has never been surpassed, stretched down before them into the garden which nestled at their feet.

Farther on rose the mighty walls of the citadel, and beyond them stretched the flower-bedecked prairies that ran off to the towering mountains twenty-five miles away.

On either side of the city ran the clear waters of

the famed Choaspes. In the gardens around the palace, palms and pomegranate trees lifted their graceful plumes, and the song of a thousand birds was borne to them on a perfume-laden breeze.

"How sweet it is!" Hanani cried, turning to Nehe. "It does not seem as if sorrow could come to us on such a day."

"And yet," Nehe added, "it was on just such a morning as this that hundreds of Jewish captives, chained by their wrists, walked two and two down yonder road, sad-hearted prisoners, gracing the triumph of the great king Nebuchadnezzar."

"I pray the God of our fathers," said Hanani, "that never again will a captive Jewish nation be led through this valley, beautiful though it may be."

"I join your prayer," said Nehe, reverently.

A slight sound attracted their attention, and, turning, the brothers saw Adna, whose pale face and drawn look showed that he, too, had passed a night of terror.

"My lord," he said, bowing respectfully, but with trembling lips, "Eros, the queen's eunuch, awaits you with a message from the king."

Nehe's expressive face paled as he leaned for a moment against one of the massive marble pillars which supported the portico, and then, with a swift, upward look, he said: —

"Let him come hither. I await the king's message."

In a moment, Eros, bearing the tray whereon rested the king's golden cup, approached Nehe.

"My lord," he said, "the queen Damaspia returns the cup, and the king commands your attendance in the audience hall this morning."

A look of infinite relief swept over Nehe's face.

"Is all well, Eros?" he asked, his voice faltering.

"All is well, my lord," replied the eunuch. "And the king further commands the presence of thy nephew, the child Bani. Since he has become 'the king's eyes,' the king would reward him this morning."

"With what, Eros?" asked Nehe.

"With a portion of the riches and honor that belonged to the dead eunuch, Barras."

"Barras dead!" Nehe exclaimed.

"No," answered Eros; "but he is dying by the boat, and the king, as is the custom, will distribute his wealth among those who have served his Majesty well."

So saying, Eros bowed and departed.

As the messenger withdrew, the brothers clasped hands.

"The Lord God be thanked!" Hanani cried; and Nehe added: "Thanks be to His name!"

"Thanks indeed!" a sweet voice echoed, as the Lady Sarai stepped out on the porch, leaning on Lydia's arm, and advanced rapidly toward them, her sweet face pale with its vigil of the night before, but bright with an unutterable look of love and happiness.

"Oh, my son," she cried, taking Nehe in her arms, "God be thanked you are safe! Surely for some great work have you escaped the snare set for you."

"For the salvation of many has he been saved, I think, mother," Hanani interposed, tenderly kissing her. "What a night of terror this has been!"

"A terrible night, indeed," Lady Sarai echoed; "but we will try to forget it now and remember only the joy of your coming."

"But, mother," protested Nehe, "will you not tell us all that happened last night in the queen's apartment?"

"No, no; not now," answered Lady Sarai, her beautiful face clouding and her eyes filling with tears. "I cannot bear even to think of it yet. But if you would hear the story, I think Ádna can give it to you."

And her smiling glance rested on the young armorbearer, who was standing beside Lydia, and leaning on a crenellated parapet of the portico, gazing into her face, while she related in low tones the scenes that took place in the queen's chamber the night before.

"This is to be a great fête day at court," Nehe said, following his mother's smiling glance, "and, as my small nephew has been summoned to an audience with the king, I must hasten to prepare him."

"What meant the eunuch by calling Bani, 'the king's eyes'?" Hanani asked anxiously. "Are you sure no harm will come to the child by this audience, my brother?"

"None, I pray," Nehe answered. "To be the king's eyes is merely this: Every Persian monarch has trusted and tried men whose sole business it is to go about among the people and see and hear what is going on, and report it to the king. To be the 'king's eyes' is to occupy an important position. The king has intended a jest, and at the same time he would honor little Bani."

"The queen told me that the king would see the darling to-day," Lady Sarai said. "Look, I have brought him a little silken robe and an embroidered scarf, and I will go myself and bathe and dress him, and teach him the prostration."

"Oh, that reminds me, mother," said Nehe, "could you spare Lydia to take charge of Bani when his father joins the tribute procession? It was to march to-day, but so many audiences are to be granted that I doubt if it will take place before to-morrow. Adna can guard them both, and they can stand on the large portico as the procession sweeps past."

"Of course I can spare her," Lady Sarai replied. "Lydia, do you come now and help me to dress Bani; and list, my maid! When you are on the portico, as you value your life and love and honor, lift not your veil in the presence of the king."

Lydia turned startled eyes on her mistress as she bowed assent, and then followed Lady Sarai, as after a long, lingering embrace to each of her handsome sons, she hastened away, and they, too, entered the palace to eat a hasty breakfast and make a careful toilet before taking Bani to the king.

CHAPTER IX

AS the brothers ate their simple breakfast of pulse and fruit, Nehe explained to Hanani the programme of the day.

"Three audiences will be given by the king," he said. "The first is for the foreign ambassadors, and also for those who would make petition of Artaxerxes. This audience will be given in the great throne room, and those attending it will only see the king; they are not expected to speak to him, save through heralds. When this audience is over, Artaxerxes receives his kinsfolk and the princes of the Seven Families in his own room or in the throne room, just as he prefers. It is then he will see Bani."

"Shall I be allowed to go in, also?" Hanani asked.

"Yes; the audience will be large, for all the Seven Nobles will give their opinion concerning the war in Egypt, and the amount that Greece ought to pay Persia as an indemnity for the part she has taken in it."

"Who are the Seven Nobles, Nehe?" Hanani asked.

"They are the heads of the seven privileged families of Persia," Nehe explained. "When Cyrus, the founder of our great empire, died, he left two sons, Smerdis and Cambyses. To Cambyses was given the kingdom, but so tormented was he with jealousy of his younger brother, that he caused him to be secretly put to death. The fact was known to but few. Cambyses then went on a campaign to Egypt, and remained away so long that he became very unpopular at home. This gave an opportunity to an impostor to impersonate the murdered Smerdis, which he did so successfully, being greatly aided by the Magian priests, that he was acknowledged by the Persians to be their ruler, and took possession of the capital. Cambyses was returning in triumph, when word was brought to him of what had happened. Overwhelmed with disgust and despair, he threw himself on his sword and died. This left the field clear to the impostor, and for a time he carried everything before him, the greatest harm to the Persians being his introduction of the impure religion of the Magi; but he lived in constant fear of detection, and took such severe measures to prevent it, that he would not allow himself to be seen by any of his nobles, nor permit any of his wives to see any one from the outside world."

"I thought that Persian kings never allowed their

wives to see anybody from the outside world," said
Hanani.

"Up to this time the king's wives had been per-
mitted to see their own relatives," Nehe answered;
"but this impostor ordered their entire seclusion.
Notwithstanding all his precautions, or perhaps on
account of them, first one and then another of the
nobles suspected him. At last suspicion grew to cer-
tainty, and word was sent to Darius, a grandson of
Cyrus, asking him to come and head a conspiracy
against the wrongful holder of the crown. He came,
raised an army, rushed into the palace, killed the impostor, and was made king. In recognition of their
services, Darius made the seven nobles his council
and elevated their families to the leading rank in the
kingdom, making it a law that Persian monarchs
must choose their wives from these families."

"This history is very interesting," said Hanani,
"but you said there would be three audiences to-day;
is it at the third that I am to present the ass that I
have brought for the king?" I am very anxious.

"Yes," replied Nehe; "this is the time when all
tribute is paid. The audience will be on the portico of
the throne room. And now I will turn you over to
Adna. He will furnish you with suitable apparel, and
tell you what is expected of you. I will come back

presently, and we will go to the audience together."

A few minutes before the water clock marked the hour of nine, the two brothers, with Bani and their attendants, ascended the steps that led into that beautiful hall whose fame has come down the centuries, the audience hall of the magnificent palace that Darius built at Susa, and on which his grandson, Artaxerxes, had spent years of labor and a princely fortune, making it the largest and most magnificent hall in all the world.

The sun, even at this early hour, would have been intensely hot, had not its heat been tempered by the cooling breezes that swept from the snow-covered mountains of Lusitan. As it was, it lit up the splendor of the magnificent portico one hundred and fifty feet long and thirty feet wide, on which the hall opened, and on the floor of which were seated groups of guards off duty, and those who were to have audience with the king later. The brilliant red and black tiling of the porch formed a pleasing background for the light Oriental costumes of the waiting crowd, and Hanani noticed again with pleasure the respectful salutations and prostrations of those whom they passed. Crossing the portico, an attendant raised for them one of the curtains that separated the porch from the hall, and Hanani stopped for a moment to gaze with wonder on the marvellous colors of the drapery — purple and scarlet, yellow and blue. They were made of exquisitely embroidered silk strips, joined by rows of network, hanging from rods of gold set in sockets attached to the pillars.

To keep them from swaying in the breeze, and so disclosing to the throng on the porch the mysterious beauty of the room within, a long, glittering fringe of golden flowers was attached to their lower edge. Beside each curtain stood a page dressed in blue, whose sole duty was to attend to his own curtain.

As they entered, Hanani's eyes were dazzled for a moment by the gorgeousness of the room, and his senses reeled as the strong, sweet odor of the perfumes burning in a hundred silver censers greeted him. Then he recovered himself and stood gazing at the magnificent scene. Architect and sculptor, painter and workman, had here joined hands to make a room fit for a god; for so the Persians held the man whose throne stood at the far end of those ranks of golden pillars which raised their heads seventy feet in the air, upholding a ceiling of blue and silver.

A subdued radiance filled the room, and at first it seemed hard to separate the blue-tiled floor overlaid with lovely rugs, from the golden walls hung with gorgeous tapestries of silk and linen, and the shining roof above.

Hanani had once stood on a mountain peak, while above and below him rolled the sunset clouds, aglow with light and life and color. He remembered the scene now, and it seemed as if he were again standing there, so penetrating was the exquisite beauty of the room. He was recalled to himself by Nehe's voice saying: —

'Have a care for your feet, brother! This carpet that leads so gracefully to yonder throne is meant for the king alone. A hundred eyes are watching you, and should your foot or Bani's touch it, death would be your punishment."

"It is a dangerous place for a child," Hanani answered anxiously, and starting back from the edge of the carpet. "Shall we not go hence?"

"It is dangerous for any one to come into the presence of a monarch," Nehe whispered back. "Every one of these proud nobles knows that his body to-night may be hanging on a cross by the roadside, if he shall offend by word or look our gracious king. This fear is the price we all pay, my brother, for our high positions."

"Then let us hasten away," Hanani protested, his fear for the child again rising.

"I must first teach him how to prostrate himself
when the king summons him," Nehe said. "Sit on
this couch, Hanani, while I do it, and look about you.
The king will not be here for some time yet. I shall
take you back to the porch before then."

As they talked, the little party moved nearer the
throne, and Nehe seated his brother on a gorgeous
couch inlaid with gold and ivory, and covered with
a magnificent embroidered robe, while he took Bani
to the steps that led up to the throne, and showed
him how to bow so low that his forehead touched
the floor. As he did so, Hanani studied the throne,
which stood a few feet away.

The throne itself was an elevated seat of gold, having a high back, but no arms, and cushioned with a
purple velvet cushion embroidered with diamonds,
pearls, and rubies. So high was the seat, a magnificent golden stool was needed to support the monarch's feet, and the whole rested on a carpet so lovely
that it was itself worth a kingdom.

The chair and stool stood on a marble slab of exquisite workmanship. The slab was upheld by the
strong arms of fourteen figures, each of which repre-
sented a nation that had been conquered by the
Persians. A sumptuous canopy of embroidered silk
dropped its soft purple folds above the throne, and

was upheld by pillars of gold encrusted with priceless jewels.

The different attendants of the king were rapidly coming in and taking the positions assigned to them by the court chamberlain. Long rows of scarlet-kilted guards were being stationed around the room, and magnificently dressed nobles were beginning to place themselves before the throne.

Arbaces stood just in front, holding the king's cup, ready to give it to Nehe when he finished Bani's lesson. Near him was the king's handkerchief-bearer and fly-chaser, whose business it was to keep flies away from the monarch. In his hand he carried a springy brush with a golden handle. The stool-carrier stood near him, and the bow-and-quiver-bearer was just behind.

A band of musicians came swiftly in, took up a position in the hall opposite the throne, and began rapidly tuning their harps. Soldiers in steel armor, with glittering swords and long cruel bows, were scattered all over the apartment, and lords and attendants in waiting, clad in gorgeous purple and crimson embroidered robes, sweet with the scent of exquisite perfumes, moved noiselessly over the shining floor, or, forming little groups, talked in low tones with one another.

Suddenly a long, clear trumpet call rang through the room, and Nehe turned and hurriedly approached Hanani.

"Come, brother," he said, "I will place you on the porch where you can see the audience of the ambassadors. After that is over, you are to follow Adna, who will bring you back, and you can watch the king receive Bani. Do just as the others do."

So saying, he led Hanani out to the portico. When they arrived there they saw that the porch was crowded with soldiers and attendants, who were rapidly placing the foreign ambassadors that were to be granted an audience. These ambassadors came from many nations. Some of them had spent weary months and encountered untold dangers, as they traversed mountain and desert and sea for this short interview with the Persian monarch. Stately Greeks from Attica, black men from mysterious Ethiopia, men from Hyrcania, Parthia, and Margiana, Scythians from the mountains of the north, — all were here, waiting for the awful moment when they could see the face of him whose hand they had long felt.

Hastily instructing Hanani where to kneel, Nehe withdrew, first stopping to give a farewell word of caution to Adna, whose handsome face wore a haughty smile, as he surveyed the mixed multitude around him. Scarcely had Nehe left, when another long trumpet call fell on the ears of the waiting expectant throng, and the whole multitude on the porch flung themselves prostrate on their faces before the long, glittering curtain that shut out the audience hall.

And now a burst of wild but majestic music comes from the hall. Louder and louder it swells, as sackbut and psaltery, harp, horn, and symphonia join their notes together in praise of him who is taking his seat within. For a few moments the music swells and crashes around them, and then dies away in a long, soft wail, and perfect stillness falls on that prostrate multitude. Silent and motionless they lie, — as silent and motionless as the huge bulls' heads that gaze with stony eyes from the height of a hundred pillars on the scene below.

Now a soft rustle is heard, and slowly, gracefully, the silken curtains are being raised, and the hushed multitude look with straining eyes on the gorgeous scene disclosed to their wondering vision. At the far end of that wilderness of marble columns, still as though carved from stone, surrounded by nobles, eunuchs, soldiers, and attendants, sits the figure of a man, so resplendent in purple and gold and jewels, so magnificent in carriage, so huge in size, that the waiting suppliants are impelled to crouch still lower on the marble floor, and from henceforth they will vow that they have seen a god.

Another long, soft call from the trumpets, and a herald, dressed in a flowing robe of blue, comes swiftly forward from the motionless ranks around the throne, and, addressing the prostrate multitude, cries in a loud, clear voice: —

"Have any here requests to make of the King Artaxerxes Longimanus? Have any here complaint to urge?"

A deep silence follows his words. Every one of the kneeling ambassadors has come with a message for that glittering figure that sits there in far-away splendor, but requests that seemed so urgent, and wrongs that seemed so grievous in distant homes, melt to insignificance now, and each waits for the other to speak. Again comes the herald's demand, and then a tall and stately Greek, in his flowing robe of white, rises and stands with his hands folded meekly on his breast; but there is a ring of haughty defiance in his voice as he gives his message to the herald.

"Water and earth Attica pays to the great King Artaxerxes; our continental cities should not longer give heavier tribute. I come to ask that what they now pay be somewhat remitted."

The herald bowed, and, holding his staff of office before him, walked swiftly back to the king. Soon he returned with the reply: —

"King Artaxerxes sends greeting to the Greeks: So long it is since the messenger left his home, perhaps he does not know that the Grecian ships that were sent to help Egypt have been captured and destroyed. Hence let him return with his request ungranted, and if he for a moment doubts the power of Persia to exact tribute, let him cast his eyes on the figures that uphold the king's throne, and then he will understand."

The Greek looked at the fourteen statues, representing the nations that Persia had conquered, and again fell prostrate in silence to the floor. Once more the herald's voice rang clear and distinct, and a native Persian rose and stood as the Greek had done, with bowed head and folded hands.

"What is it the suppliant wishes?" the herald asked. And with beating heart and downcast eyes, the man answered:—

"May the king live forever, and know that his servant owned, in the outskirts of the city, a little plot of ground next to the estate of his great lord, Arkano. I am, O king, a chariot-driver, and in the last great war with Egypt was away from my home a year. When I returned, I found that Arkano had given out that I was dead. He had seized my children claiming I owed him a debt, and had sold them and my wife into slavery. Justice I ask, O king! Justice, on this my enemy!"

The herald retired as before, and returned, saying: "The king has ordered that the case be examined into, and if it be as reported, let the noble Arkano give to the man a sufficient sum that he may purchase another wife."

The suppliant did not seem satisfied with the king's decision, for, trembling violently, and bowing still lower, he murmured: —

"Arkano did not rest, my lord, with taking my wife and children, but he seized the plot of ground wherein were the tombs of my ancestors, and added it to his pleasure garden."

The second appeal affected the king far more than the first, for the herald returned with the answer: —

"The king has said: 'If this be true, Arkano must be punished. It is easy enough for the living to care for themselves, but it is the duty of every brave man to care for the dead. Tell him to go, and if this charge be true, his own wife and children shall be returned to him, for if the crime of desecrating the abodes of the dead be continued, who knows how long the

tombs of the kings themselves will be safe! And
Arkano shall make restitution of the sepulchres of his
ancestors and punishment be meted out to him."

The man bowed humbly, and with a glad look
prostrated himself once more, while to Nehe, standing near the throne, came a happy thought, and he
whispered to himself: —

"I know how to make my plea! I know how to
reach the king's heart!"

A few other requests were made, and then the
silken curtains were dropped and the audience was
over.

CHAPTER X

AS the crowd of suppliants quietly dispersed Nehe returned to the porch, and led Hanani into the audience hall.

"The king has gone to his own apartments," he explained, "but he will soon return. Stand here by this pillar, Hanani, and remember, my brother, that strange and possibly terrible things may take place before your eyes; but whatever befalls, keep your tongue silent and your face smiling."

As he spoke, the sound of approaching music was heard, and in an instant every one in the vast audience hall, save the guards, fell prostrate on the floor. Hanani and Bani prostrated themselves with the rest, and as they lay there the music came nearer and nearer. Then was heard the tread of many feet. The harpers in the hall burst forth into a triumphant melody, and Hanani knew that the mighty King Artaxerxes Longimanus, ruler of Persia, was passing by. The music swept along, and Hanani ventured, without raising himself, to lift his head enough to observe what was going on around him. The harpers, still singing and playing, had taken up a position back of the throne, and on this the king had now seated himself.

When Hanani had been on the porch, the distance was too great for him to see the king distinctly, but he now saw that the monarch was a very tall, handsome man, with long, graceful hands, whose size and strength had won for him the title Longimanus, or long-handed. His hair was curled in a hundred stiff and rather short curls, that hung down on his neck, and his long beard was arranged in the same curious fashion. On his head was the high stiff hat of purple felt worn only by kings. His dress was a magnificent robe of purple silk, embroidered in gold, and confined at the waist by a broad gold belt. This robe opened over a tight-fitting tunic of purple and white silk, also exquisitely embroidered. He wore high, soft shoes, yellow in color, and fastened with buttons, each button a gem of great value.

In his hand the king held a long golden sceptre; and, as he sat resting its point on the velvet carpet in front of him, Hanani trembled as he remembered that if any one came toward him and it was not lifted, the unhappy man or woman would be hurried away to instant death. So completely, so absolutely, did the ancient monarchs hold the lives of their subjects.

Then his mind went back to his own country of

Judea, and as he remembered how free and happy its
people once were, how even the great King David
himself could not condemn a man to death without
just cause, he wondered why its people could ever
have longed to be like the heathen nations. But he
dismissed the thought as quickly as it came, and fixed
his gaze on the wonderful scene before him.

As the king sat down, his umbrella-bearer, holding
a small umbrella of yellow silk, took up his station
directly behind him. His fan-bearer, waving a huge
fan of peacock feathers, stood beside him. Nehe, advancing, knelt at his feet, holding up the golden cup,
now filled with delicious wine. His bow-bearer also
drew near, and stationed himself directly behind the
king. Every one in the hall save the officers still
knelt, but at a signal from the king all now arose and
stood with their hands folded on their breasts, in
token of abject submission. The king's piercing eye
swept the room, and lighted on Bani, who stood with
his hand clinging to Adna's robe.

As he saw him, King Artaxerxes turned to Nehe:

"Tell me, my gallant cup-bearer," he said, "is it to
yonder child I owe the fact that I have a cup-bearer
this morning? For I do think the trick of Barras
would have succeeded had not the boy tasted the
cup."

"He is my nephew," Nehe answered, "and the child who found the poison."

The king raised his glittering sceptre until its end pointed directly toward Bani.

"Bring him here," he said. "We have a small present for him."

Adna led Bani forward, and he knelt before the king, as he had been taught, shaking back his long, fair curls and smiling up into the king's face.

"A goodly child," said Artaxerxes, carelessly. "Harbana," turning to the nobleman who stood near, "give him of the treasure you found in Barras's treasure chest."

Harbana advanced, and poured into the robe of Bani a quantity of gold coins, and beautiful gems engraved in various designs.

"There, my small Eyes," the king said, laughing, "now give place to my next petitioner."

Bani struggled to his feet, his lovely face beaming with delight over his lapful of pretty things, and holding tight to the edges of his robe, as Adna led him back to his father.

"He will make a fine fellow," the king said admiringly, while he watched Bani's sturdy little figure as he held up his treasures for Hanani to see. "Is he old enough to take from his mother?"

"He is of the age at which Persian boys are taken from their mothers," Nehe replied, "but, alas! this boy has no mother. His father is a native of Jerusalem, and the Samaritan, Sanballat, has stolen his wife and holds her captive."

"Is it so?" said the king; "then select another wife for him. A bevy of maidens of unusual loveliness have just been brought into the palace for me to select from for the royal harem. When I have finished choosing to-morrow, let your brother take from the remainder a wife for himself and a mother for the child, if he will."

Nehe bowed, and the king continued: —

"I know these maids are beautiful, though I sometimes think that Harbana is losing his eye for beauty, when I see the ones he brings me."

The chamberlain turned pale at the jest of the king, who continued good-naturedly: —

"But these, I know, are lovely, for many of them come from the tribe of Pæonians. Heard you ever of them, my Nehe?"

"I think not, my lord king."

Artaxerxes laughed.

"The story is an entertaining one. You shall hear it. Bring hither the scroll, Harbana."

The nobleman hastened away and soon returned

with a cylinder of richly engraved silver. Opening it, he took out a scroll of papyrus, which he unrolled and then read aloud: —

"Chronicles of the Life of King Darius. Behold, as the king sat one day on his throne in a strange city, a woman of great stature passed him, arranged in flowing garments of richest silk. Her long, brown hair fell like a veil around her radiant face. On her head she bore a pitcher. With her arm she led a horse, and with her hand she spun flax as she went. So intent was the maid, she did not even regard the king himself as she passed by. 'Follow the woman!' commanded King Darius, 'for never saw I so industrious and beautiful a being before.' The guard followed her, and behold, when she reached the river, first she watered her horse, then she filled her pitcher, and then returned, spinning her flax as she walked. When this matter was repeated to the king, he marvelled greatly and asked to what nation she belonged, and when they told him, 'To the Pæonian?' he said: 'Then let all the Pæonian nation be at once transported to Persia, for I would teach our women how they can be at the same time beautiful and industrious.' So came the Pæonians into Asia."

"A goodly story," smiled the king, as Harbana finished reading. "Have it put on brick, and added to the chronicles of the king in the citadel. Your brother could not have a better choice of a maid for a wife."

Again Nehe bowed, but a bitter thought came into the listening Hanani's mind: —

"If the king could dismiss so lightly the loss of my wife, Nehe was right that it would be useless to plead this as a reason for rebuilding the walls of Jerusalem."

A moment afterward, Hatach, the head of one of the seven privileged families, advanced to the throne, and began making arrangements for a lion hunt which was to take place next day.

"Thy last shot, Artaxerxes," he said courteously, "where you killed the lion even as he sprang forward, was the most wonderful feat of archery ever done by Persian king!"

"I can do as well again," the king answered enthusiastically. "Harbana, give me my bow, and I will show you, Hatach, that I can shoot as well to-day."

His bow-bearer handed him his bow, and Artaxerxes began looking for a target. As his eye glanced restlessly around the room, many a page in waiting trembled, for they well remembered that at his last trial of skill he had chosen the heart of one of their number as his target, and struck it so straight and true the boy had died without a struggle.

Now, however, his glance left them and rested on little Bani, who was sitting with his back against a pillar, playing with the jewels the king had just given him.

"There," he said, "I was just about as far from the lion as from yonder child. See, I will aim at his eyes. Give me my bow."

The bow-bearer stepped forward and handed Artaxerxes the bow and a long, sharp-pointed arrow. The king fitted the latter in place, and took long, careful aim at Bani's eyes, but just as he drew the string the child turned his head, and the king's aim was spoiled.

Nehe had stood trembling with horror. The danger to Bani had come so suddenly that he was totally unprepared for it, and he had gazed on the king as if fascinated; but when the child moved, the spell that held his tongue was broken, and, bowing low, he said, smiling, but knowing the words might cost him his life: —

"My lord the king, it is easy to shoot a child's big head, but see that glittering bauble in the boy's hand! Shoot that, and the story shall be told in every house in Susa to-night of the king's wonderful aim. Bani," Nehe cried, raising his strong, clear voice, "Bani, lift up your right hand, child, and hold it steady! Steady!"

The child looked at his uncle wonderingly, and then his little chubby fist lifted itself waveringly, as high as his heart, — as high as his head, — and then it paused.

"Higher, Bani, higher!" Nehe cried, smiling, but with icy fear clutching him. Would the child lift it high enough to escape the arrow King Artaxerxes was so carefully fitting to his bow? Yes, slowly the chubby, dimpled hand went up until it was quite over his head, holding the large jewel between baby fingers.

Nehe shut his eyes. He could not watch the arrow speed to its place. He could only wait.

A second later the twang of the string told him the king had shot, and then a burst of applause rang through the mighty hall. The king had knocked the jewel from Bani's grasp, and was receiving the rapturous praise of his admiring subjects.

CHAPTER XI

THAT evening Nehe and Hanani and the Lady Sarai walked together in the palace garden.

"It has been a fearful day," Hanani said. "Oh, Nehe, when I saw that arrow aimed at Bani's eyes, I wonder that I did not die of the agony that clutched me."

"And yet great good has come from it," the Lady Sarai answered. "Our little Bani will be rich for life on the treasures the king gave him, and in his far-away Jerusalem home they will be a great blessing."

"And I shall have to face that terrible king again to-morrow," said Hanani.

"I thought that the presentation of tribute was to be to-day," the Lady Sarai commented.

"So it was to be," Nehe answered, "but after the last audience, the king said he was tired, and therefore the tribute procession must be postponed until to-morrow. But do not fear, Hanani. Surely no harm can come to you in the procession."

"I fear harm whenever I think of the king or his court," Hanani declared. "Nehe, will you not hasten your errand with the king?"

"Yes," Nehe assented, "and this morning a wonderful thought came to me. I dare not go to the king to plead the cause of my living kinsmen, but I will go to plead for the graves of my ancestors, now being destroyed by the treacherous Arabs."

"The thought surely comes from God," Hanani answered; "you remember how this morning the king instantly granted justice to the man whose fathers' graves had been disturbed."

"It was that which gave me the idea," Nehe replied. "And now, my mother, do you and Hanani pray and fast forty days. I, too, will pray and fast, and at the end of the forty days I will go up to the king and make petition of him that I may go to mine own city, to rebuild its walls, that the graves of my ancestors may remain undisturbed by their enemies, and the worship of the Lord Jehovah be restored. If the king sees fit to be angry with me, I can but perish."

"We will join you in the fasting and prayer, dear Nehe," the Lady Sarai answered; "but you will not perish. Who among the Jews has ever undertaken the work of the Lord and failed? He will strengthen and uphold you, and you shall find favor in the king's eyes."

"Bravely spoken, dear mother," Hanani answered.

"I, too, believe as you do. God will not suffer a hair of his head to be touched, who is His own ambassador! But it grieves me, mother, that you must so soon lose your two sons."

"Lose them?" said the Lady Sarai, smiling; "my son, you know not what you say! I am not one to be left behind when my sons set out for mine own country. I have great wealth, too, as Nehe knows, and it shall be joined to his to help to restore the city of my fathers, our dearly beloved Jerusalem."

"But will the queen permit you?" Nehe questioned.

"I will tell her it is but for a time, and I think she will," Sarai answered.

"And I, my lady?" questioned a soft voice; and Sarai, turning, saw her handmaiden, Lydia, kneeling beside her, with the privileged freedom of a Jewish girl. "Shall I not go, too, my lady?"

"You, girl?" Sarai answered, her dark eyes looking sorrowfully into the pleading blue ones upraised to her own. "It is not to your country I go nor to your nation. You are but a heathen girl and have no part among God's chosen people."

"No, no, my lady," protested the kneeling maid; "I am not a heathen. Alas! I know not my country nor my kinsfolk, for I was so young when old Zexa stole me from my parents that I remember not their nation. But ever since I entered your service I have prayed to your God. Never once have I turned my face in worship to the eternal fires. Never have I bowed before great Ormazd, or the goddesses in the harem. But ever do I pray to the Lord God of Israel, save one short prayer which I do not understand. No, my lady, I am not as the heathen be."

And the maid raised her face, shining with girlish indignation, and looked at her mistress beseechingly. Lady Sarai turned an appealing look upon Nehe, as he said firmly but kindly: —

"Lydia, why should you follow us to Jerusalem? Do you not know that no Jew may wed any save a woman of his own nation? And," here he paused a moment, and then added quietly, "Adna is a Jew."

A great wave of color swept over the girlish face. Then she bowed herself more humbly still.

"Oh, my lord," she said, and the words were spoken so low that Nehe was obliged to bend to catch them, "I do not ask to marry him, my lord; I only ask to love him."

CHAPTER XII

WITH many admonitions and cautions, Hanani consigned Bani into Lydia's care on the following morning.

"Hold tight to Lydia's hand, Bani," he said, "and do not laugh aloud or call to me, even when you see me go by in the great procession. Keep very quiet, and you shall have ever and ever so many grapes for your dinner."

"And honey?" questioned the child, anxiously.

"Oh, yes," laughed Nehe, who was waiting while his brother spoke these last words; "as much honey as all the bees in the king's garden can steal from all the lilies to-day."

"The bees do not steal," said the child, decidedly. "The lilies give it to the bees to make Bani's teeth white like them."

And he laughed so that every pearly tooth flashed out as white from his pomegranate lips, as a lily set in rosebuds.

"I will be very careful of the child, my lord," interposed Lydia, quietly, lowering her veil, as she took Bani's hand to lead him away.

"I am sure you will, my girl," Hanani answered heartily; "but the very thought of the king makes me shudder."

"Then don't think of him, brother," laughed Nehe. "Come, we must go at once. Already the procession is forming, and soon I shall be needed. Take good care of them both, Adna, and don't forget the boy in looking after the girl."

And Nehe walked off, smiling.

Just as the young people were about to start, Bani discovered that he was hungry, and loudly demanded his milk and honey then and there. Lydia knew that all the processions in the world would be as nothing to a hungry boy; so the bread and milk and honey were sent for, and Bani leisurely ate them. When he had finished, Adna hurried the little party out into the court, and then, seeing the crowd, exclaimed: —

"It is too bad, Lydia! The king has already come out upon the portico of the throne room. We cannot go up the marble steps."

"What shall we do, then?" the girl asked anxiously.

"We can go up the private roadway that the king's chariot uses. It winds around the walls to the top. But let us hurry! The procession will surely start soon."

Hastening their footsteps, the party soon reached the portico and, stopping, gazed with keen interest upon the scene below. Lydia had been there before, but in spite of that she gave a little cry of delight, as Adna placed her against a pillar and told her to look around.

In the centre of the portico itself stood a magnificent high chair of gold, and on this sat the king, ablaze with jewels, and surrounded by his officers and guards. All the curtains of the throne room were raised, so that the magnificence of that apartment formed a gorgeous background for his royal person. Before him ran four flights of polished stone steps, leading to the court below. They were clear of visitors now, and the beauty of the gray stone steps, which were so wide that ten horsemen could ride abreast up their shining surface, reflected back the sculptured ranks of stone figures that seemed to be ascending their sides, all aglow with the brilliant colors of their living models which were now entering the court below. High above the portico towered golden pillars upholding the roof, and each end of the porch was guarded by gigantic stone bulls.

As the king sat there, he looked down into the court, over the tiled floor of which was already beginning to move the long train of tribute-bearers, who had assembled in the plain without, their holiday dresses adding to the beauty of the already lovely scene. Stately buildings reared their proud heads all around the court, their airy pillars covered with delicate tracery and gleaming with decorations of bronze and gold and silver, shining through trees of every shade of green. Fountains splashed in gardens whose beds of many-hued flowers were so united by tiled walks of blue and pink, that from the portico they looked like huge bouquets tied together with bright ribbons. Everywhere the eye turned it was delighted with the wealth of lovely form and color, glowing in the clear air of that matchless climate. And the great king, looking down on it all, knew that nowhere else in the world could there be so magnificent a scene as this which lay before him.

Lydia turned to Adna. "How lovely it all is," she said. "See, the procession is starting, is it not? Who leads the way?"

Adna stooped and lifted little Bani in his arms, so that the child could see over the heads of the many inmates of the palace gathered on the portico, and then looked in the direction Lydia pointed.

"Yes, it is starting," he answered, "and, as usual, the king's guard comes first."

As he spoke a blare of instruments struck their

ears, and the head of the procession began making
its way up the easy ascent of the first flight of stairs.
The king's guard, as the company of soldiers that
led the way was called, was composed of spearmen
and archers. The former were armed with spears and
slings, and were men of very unusual height and
strength. They carried large shields of polished brass
engraved with a representation of the Susanian
fortress. Back of them came the archers, who were
not so large as the spearmen, but seemed to be more
agile. Their graceful forms were the perfection of
muscular development. Their long, tight gowns were
of purple linen, embroidered all over with golden
pictures of the crenellated walls of Susa. Their hair
was tightly curled, and so were their beards, and
large quivers, elaborately ornamented, were strapped
to their backs with cords of gold. Yellow shoes covered their feet, and they advanced swiftly, with the
proud bearing of men who knew that they would win
praise from the haughty eyes of the silent figure before whom they filed.

After the king's guard came the noblemen of the
court, the kinsmen of the monarch, chamberlains and
heads of departments, those who held the king dearest, and who would most mourn his death. These
were his living wall, without which he never went to

battle. High, square tiaras crowned each proud head, and magnificent robes of silk, clustered with jewels and embroidery, decked their forms. Each carried in his hand a rose, to show that no tribute was exacted of him save that rendered by love.

Sandwiched in between these nobles in their costly array were hardy mountaineers, clad in close-fitting tunics and baggy trousers of leather. They, too, carried no rich tribute, but only a flower to show that they, as well as the haughty noblemen beside whom they walked, were the king's own free people.

And now came the chamberlains of the king, each individual clad in his robe of state, and bearing no weapon save his staff of office, and leading by the hand a tribute-bearer. What a mixed multitude they made as they swept up those glistening stairs, past the king, and down the outside steps, in long, unbroken ranks! Who can imagine this procession of tribute-bearers, bringing to this monarch whom they thought was half-god, half-man, the treasures of their countries? Here came a poor African, looking half-dazed as the gorgeous chamberlain led him along, his huge black frame clothed only in a cotton breech-cloth, and bearing in his arms a large tusk of ivory. Behind him walked the pearl-fishers, carrying earthen vessels filled with the purest pearls. From distant

Greek cities in Asia came slender youths, their white
costumes not more stainless than the exquisite vases
of rarest marble they bore. Behind them walked the
keen-eyed, black-haired sons of the desert, looking
out from beneath their turbans in fierce disdain of
all this pent-up splendor, leading softly stepping
steeds whose pure blood for generations had been as
carefully guarded as was that of the Achæmenidæ
themselves. Heavy-browed Egyptians carried costly
vases filled with perfume so precious that each drop
was worth a man's ransom; and rugged forms of
mountaineers bowed beneath the weight of magnificent leopard skins. Miners from distant Datum
laden with balls of pure gold as large as their heads
were followed by men bearing scales, so that the king
might know the exact weight of the shining globes,
should he be curious on that point. From Babylon
came high-browed, straight-nosed, clean-limbed men,
weighted with rolls of costly cotton fabrics, colored as
only the Babylonians knew how to dye cotton goods.
Chariots covered with expensive trappings of gold
and silver embroidery were there, and close after
them walked a dusky hunter who had killed a great
tiger. He had thrown its tawny skin over himself
for a covering, and his frightened face looked out
appealingly to the king oddly enough from beneath

the fierce head of the beast. This sight excited Bani's wonder. He was quite close to Lydia as Adna held him, and he grasped her veil to attract her attention.

"Look, look, Lydia!" he exclaimed. "See the man with two heads!"

And he jerked the veil impatiently to make her turn more quickly. As the child did so, he loosened it, and the veil fell from the maiden's head.

"Oh," cried the girl, in dismay, turning laughing but half-frightened eyes to Adna, "what would my lady say if she saw me now?"

"That you were never half so fair," Adna whispered back; "but hasten, Lydia, to replace it."

The girl lifted her bare, snowy arms to do his bidding, just as Hanani, leading the white ass, came in sight.

"I see you, father!" shrieked Bani, fairly wild with excitement. "See, see! Here's me!"

The clear, childish voice floated over the heads of the crowd, and many an eye was turned to see from whence came the eager cry. The king had been sitting for some time listlessly watching the procession, occasionally commenting to his cup-bearer on an unusually rich gift, but generally as silent and impassive as the carved figures on the sculptured stairway; but at the cry of the child he turned his head, and his eye caught the eager face of Bani, framed in its bright ringlets.

"Ah," he said, "there is my little Eyes,—a goodly child, a goodly child."

Then his glance fell on the upturned face of Lydia, as with trembling haste she strove to cover it with her long veil. Not quick enough were the kindly folds to shut out from the gaze of the monarch that wealth of golden hair, falling like a shining veil around her, those eyes blue as the skies above them, those frightened, rose-red lips, — and the king's face brightened as he caught that glimpse of girlish beauty.

"Nehe," he said, as he pointed to Lydia, "did I not say that Harbana does not know a beautiful maid when he sees one? Else why was not this girl included in those selected for the royal harem? See to it that she be sent in with the next who come."

Nehe bowed, smiling, but a faint, sick feeling filled him, and he thought: —

"Poor little Lydia! Poor brave Adna! How soon their love dream must be shattered! And yet perhaps it were better so. Adna could not marry her. He must not. He is a Jew."

Already Nehe was troubled concerning the disposition to be made of the girl if his mother should leave Susa. Now the question was settled. She would be in the harem of the king, — a living death to one of her loving nature, and yet what could avert her fate?

The tide of the procession swept on. Battleaxes from Greece, Persian carpets from the monarch's own cities, strange wild animals for the king's hunting grounds, costly garments, rare fruits and nuts for his table, and then a long, long train of captives chained two by two, walking with downcast eyes and folded hands.

But Adna no longer saw the moving figures. His eyes alternately rested on the girlish form beside him and the calm, smiling face of his master, as he filled and held out again and again the shining cup to the king.

"What was it," he repeated to himself, "what was it the king said to Nehe as he looked so long on Lydia?"

CHAPTER XIII

NIGHT was softly falling over the city of Susa, and in the queen's apartments of the harem, white-robed eunuchs moved quietly about, lighting a hundred lamps, whose soft radiance fled across the room, showing its wonderful ceiling of beams of cedar wood, overlaid with silver, and then, gliding down the walls, it brought out the glowing colors of the figures that marched in stately procession around them. It showed the heavily fringed curtains that draped the windows, and almost turned to life the forms of slaves carved on the heavy wooden doors. It lay on the blue-tiled floor, and the rugs there were changed from dark shadows to softest colors. But, fairest of all things the light showed in that apartment, furnished with statuary stolen from Greek temples, with magnificent Egyptian vases, with couches covered with robes heavy with embroidery, was the lovely Queen Damaspia herself.

She was reclining on a low seat of ivory, beside a fountain of perfumed water, one dimpled arm stretched along its marble edge, while the other circled the head of a tiny fawn that was cuddled against her. Her gown was of that material made by the Egyptians, and so exquisitely fine the Persians called it woven air. It was embroidered with roses, and so thin was the material on which they were set, the queen as she lay there looked as if clothed in wreaths of living flowers.

A beautiful girl stood behind the queen, fanning her with a large fan of peacock feathers. Other maids were looping back the heavy silk curtains that shut out the soft, balmy air, and others were sprinkling flower petals over the rugs, singing a soft song as they did so.

Facing the queen sat an elderly woman, whose robe of heavy silk was so beautifully embroidered it seemed as if trying to draw and hold one's eyes away from the face of the wearer. A cruel, wrinkled, wicked face it was, so plainly had sin and treachery and deception marked it. One was glad to turn from it to the pretty, laughing countenance of the queen opposite.

The slaves had scarcely finished lighting the lamps, when the door opened and the king appeared, carrying in his hand not a sceptre of power, but that of love — a rose. Both women stood up as he entered, but he advanced to the elder first and gravely saluted her, and then turned to the queen.

"Come, Damaspia," he said; "see, I have here a rope of purest pearls, fit for thy fair neck, and a vase engraved from a single emerald by one of those wonderful Greeks. I am willing to risk them both on the throw of the dice. Now, what can you offer as your wager?"

The queen looked around the apartment.

"I will wager you yon fat eunuch," she said. "No one in Persia can mix wine and honey and cool it as can he; but you shall have him, if your rope of pearls is as lovely as you say."

"Bring hither the vase and pearls," the king said, turning to one of the eunuchs who had entered with him; and the man instantly handed to him a casket of richly engraved silver. "There are the pearls," the king added, as he opened it; "and here is the vase," and he set a glittering jewel on the fountain's rim beside Damaspia.

The queen uttered a cry of delight and clapped her hands.

"How lovely they are! See, mother," she said, lifting the long string of shimmering pearls, and holding them toward the woman who faced her. "Saw you ever a more perfect rope?"

"Never, save this," answered the old woman, touching as she spoke a shining row of pearls that girdled her waist; "but I do not care to look at trinkets now. I am thinking and planning."

"Of what are you thinking, mother queen?" the king asked pleasantly, as he smiled at the delight of Damaspia over her pearls.

"Of which is the worst punishment," the queen mother answered, her deep-set eyes sparkling maliciously. "Which would you rather, Damaspia, have your pretty ears and nose and mouth cut off and your tongue torn out, or be buried alive?"

Damaspia gave a little cry, and shot a frightened glance at the king as she answered: —

"Oh, Queen Amestis, why think such thoughts to-night?"

"I was just remembering," said the queen dowager. "It was thus I served Inarus when she displeased me, and I wonder if it would not have punished her more had I buried her alive."

"Come, come, mother!" cried the king, half angrily, "I will not have my dove so frightened. And he laid his jewelled hand protectingly on Damaspia. "Have the dice brought out, my queen, and let us throw."

Two attendants quickly set forward a high table of cedar wood overlaid with gold and ivory, and placed beside it the tall chairs and stools that the king and queen used when playing, while another attendant produced the dice, and then in a few moments the game began. Damaspia threw first and watched anxiously.

"Five and six," she laughed. "My lord, can you do better?"

And she laid her hand on the silver casket that had been set beside her. As she did so, stealing in from the harem garden, came the low, sweet notes of a nightingale.

"Hush," said the king, and turned to listen, for the bird's song was one of unusual beauty. Then, as the music died softly away, a human voice took up the strains the bird had sung, thrilling and trilling them over and over, at first soft and low, then louder and clearer, until at last the liquid notes crystallized into words, and the bird, catching the song, joined its voice to the maid's, and girl and bird sang together. The king listened as if entranced. His handsome features softened under the spell of the music, and a look of tender longing grew in his haughty black eyes.

How beautiful the words were the maiden was singing! Clear and true they came floating through the silken draperies, and every syllable sank into the king's heart with a sweet pain: —

> "'Behold, thou art fair, my love!
> Behold, thou art fair!
> Thou hast dove's eyes, my love;
> Thou hast dove's eyes.'"

The singer was singing the words of that matchless love song written by the wisest man that ever lived, as he painted the pure affection of one man for one woman, in colors that can never die. The singer had heard the song sung by some captive Hebrew girls, and, catching the words, she clothed them in all the beauty of her sweet, rich, tender young voice, and was pouring them forth in the harem garden, little dreaming who was listening, or the terrible harm they would do her. Even the queen stopped toying with her rope of pearls, and held her jewelled hand suspended, as the pulsing music flowed through the chamber.

> "'Set me as a seal upon thy heart, beloved,'"

ran the words,

> "'as a seal upon thine arm.'"

The king glanced at Damaspia. He had been true to her beyond all precedent. She alone could claim the honor of being his wife, but did she love him for all the wealth and tenderness he had lavished upon her? He turned and gazed searchingly into the bright eyes of the woman opposite, but no answering love-light met the tender longing of his own, and he realized, with a bitterness he had never known before, that the feeling which was being lauded out there in the garden had never been given to him. Gently, pleadingly, came the words as the singer sang: —

"'For love is strong as death.'"

And then the sweet voice grew exultant as it burst forth in an ecstasy of triumphant song: —

"'Many waters cannot quench it,
Neither can the floods drown it.'"

The music stopped abruptly, and the monarch stirred uneasily, and then turned and looked through the open draperies as if he would catch a glimpse of the unseen singer. A strong determination was growing in his heart. He, too, would know and feel this wonderful love, and yet he felt dimly that this was a gift which must be given, and that all his wealth was helpless to purchase it. And who among all the beauties that smiled around him could give him the treasure of a woman's strong, true love? Instinctively he felt that it must come from a sweet, pure soul, and, alas! it were useless to look for such here, among these heathen women whose very worship was too often a defilement.

But surely the singer who had been singing so entracingly of love could feel it. Her woman's heart must hold the treasure he was seeking, and he would win and hold it as his choicest possession. This love should be his, dearer than life itself, — this love that waters could not quench, that floods could not drown.

Never had Artaxerxes looked more manly than when, filled with the sudden resolve, he turned to Damaspia and said: —

"Who is yon singer, O queen? Among all thy singing maids, methinks I never heard so sweet a voice. Is she an inmate of the harem?"

"No," answered the queen. "The singer is but the handmaid of the Lady Sarai. She has owned her from a child, though it is but of late that she has sung such songs as this. Sarai keeps her close in her own apartment. Her name is Lydia."

"Is she not a Jew?" the monarch asked, and in his heart he hoped the answer would be yes, for he had heard strange stories told of the beauty and constancy of the Jewish women, and he knew this was true from his memory of Queen Esther, the Jewess, who was esteemed above all other women because of her love and courage. His face fell at Queen Damaspia's reply: —

"No; I think she is of no kin to Sarai — only a girl she bought for a handmaiden. But shall we not return to our game? I fancy you are afraid to cast your dice, now you have seen my high count. It was five and six, remember."

The king put out his hand mechanically for the dice and threw them.

"Four and two," laughed Damaspia. "Give me my rope of pearls, my lord. See, is it not lovely?" And she flung the milky string of gems over her head.

"Very beautiful," the king answered, smiling at her, "yet the pearls are not so white as the fair neck beneath. But I am weary to-night. We will play again to-morrow."

He pushed the high table back and arose. As he did so, the old queen leaned forward, stretching out a jewelled, bony hand to detain him.

"Son Artaxerxes," she said, "I will play you a game, and your stake shall be twelve goodly youths, and mine shall be the singer you have heard in the garden to-night. Will you throw the dice with me?"

"Yes, yes," answered Artaxerxes, and turning to an attendant, he ordered: "Place my chair and a table. I will try my luck again."

"The fair singer interests you more than the fat eunuch, my lord," Damaspia pouted. "Let us see how the dice will treat you."

The king threw first.

"Three and two," he said, discontentedly. "You have won also, I fancy, mother. I fear the god is against me to-night."

The old queen apparently did not hear him. She was busily unravelling a long, vivid-colored thread from the fringe of her cloak. Then she turned to a eunuch.

"Hold the silver lamp," she said. "I would invoke the god."

The man hastily caught up the silver hand-lamp that stood on a table near by, and the queen cast the thread into the flame, muttering as she did so: —

"'Like this dyed thread, which is torn and cast into the fire,
   The burning flame shall consume the disease which exists in
      my muscles;
   Like this dyed thread may it be torn,
   And on this day may the burning flame consume it.'"

"To whom do you pray, mother?" asked the king.

The queen drew a curiously engraved gem from her bosom and held it out to him.

"To the god of the underground regions, Pluto," she replied. "I learned his worship when I went with Xerxes on his expedition against the Greeks. Ah, I was young then, but well I remember that wondrous journey."

"I like not the worship of these strange gods,

mother," the king answered. "Ormazd is the great god. Our fathers worshipped him; so should we."

The queen laughed a malicious little laugh.

"Heard you never the tale of Xerxes at the River Nine Ways? Nine were the maidens very beautiful, nine were the youths handsome and sturdy, that he buried alive there to propitiate the god. And," she added, scowling darkly, "I would do the same."

"Nay, nay, mother! Let us have no such rites at the Persian court. Come, throw me the dice! I have but five."

The queen's jewelled hand poised in the air.

"If I win," she said insistently, "twelve youths will I offer to the god of the underground regions. Perhaps he will add all the unlived years of their lives to mine. So shall I live to see thy son and thy son's son on the throne of Persia." And she threw the dice.

With a gesture of haughty displeasure Artaxerxes leaned forward to count, and the heart of every maiden in the room beat more freely as he announced: —

"One and two. The god is with me. I have saved nine maidens, mother, and won the singer!"

Then, hastily rising, he quitted the apartment.

CHAPTER XIV

THE clepsydra marked the hour of eleven, and Lady Sarai, having finished her attendance upon the queen, was in her own room preparing for repose. She was seated on a high chair. Before her knelt a slave girl holding up a silver basin of perfumed water, while behind her stood Lydia, brushing her still long and abundant hair. The maiden's tongue ran gayly as she related the scenes of the morning, and both were laughing over the tale, when Eros, the chief eunuch, hastily entered the room, saying: —

"My lady, Harbana, the chamberlain of the court, is without, commanding the instant attendance of your handmaiden Lydia on the king."

A chill of deadly fear fell on the maiden. She shrank nearer her mistress and dropped on her knees beside her, catching hold of Sarai's robe, and turning her white flower-face to the eunuch in desperate appeal.

"Oh, Eros!" she cried, "surely your ears heard not aright. It was not I he asked for. I do not belong to the harem. The king has never seen me."

"Lydia," interposed Sarai, laying her hand protectingly on the girl's upturned forehead, "did not the king see your face when Bani pulled your veil away this morning?"

"Oh!" moaned the girl, "I fear he did; and to-night I sang in the harem gardens, unknowing that he was within. But the queen had commanded my singing. I could not help it. I did but choose my song."

"My lady," Eros interposed coldly, "the chamberlain of the king awaits Lydia."

Sarai bent forward pityingly.

"Go, dear heart," she said; "no human power can save you from the king; but pray to that God whom you have learned to serve. He may hear even a heathen maiden's prayer. I, too, will pray."

Lydia arose, and with trembling hands quickly adjusted her veil.

"I go, my lady," she said, "but never will I consent to enter the king's harem — no, not if Artaxerxes send me to death by his most terrible torture. Never, never, will I enter the king's harem!"

And with downcast eyes but with a resolute step she followed Eros from the apartment.

So great had been the heat of the day, it had penetrated even to the darkened recesses of the palace,

and the king had felt it and suffered. Remembering
this, after leaving the queen, he stopped on the portico of his own private apartments. Here he sat,
attended only by Nehe, Adna, and his armor-bearer;
under the quiet canopy of the stars, breathing the
cool night breeze, and listening to the soft swish of
the water that was throwing up silvery arms in the
moonlight, against the brick walls of the fortress
fifty feet below. Into this little group, Eros and
Harbana ushered Lydia. Her graceful white-robed
form came so quietly among them, it seemed as if
she might have floated up from the mist of the river
below.

The king was seated, as usual, on a high chair,
while around him stood the other men. His face
wore a look of good-natured expectancy. Evidently
he was about to bestow a boon, which would give as
great pleasure to the recipient as to the giver. As
Lydia advanced and knelt before him, he put out his
hand to raise her.

"Girl," he asked, "are you she who sang so
sweetly of love in yonder garden to-night?"

Lydia arose, trembling, but no answer came from
her closed lips. Through her unlifted veil she looked
at the group around the king. They were all smiling
at her, but only the king spoke: —

"Answer me, maid," he said. "You little knew that your song to-night opened the gate to the king's heart, and you entered in. There you may find such love as that of which you sang, for he stands ready to give it to you. Can you understand that, girl? We saw your face, sweet as a blossom, this morning, and its loveliness lingered with us all the day. Resolute it is, too, as that of the angel Serosh. Raise your veil, my maid! Let me again drink in your loveliness."

Lydia drew back her veil, and the king uttered an exclamation of surprise.

"Why are you so pale, child? Where are all those roses fled? And your eyes! Banish that frightened look! We are all friends here."

Lydia raised her beautiful eyes and glanced again at the group. The king looked at her, smiling still. And then she saw Nehe's face, kindly compassionate, and then a wave of crimson swept over her as her eyes met Adna's. He had stepped behind the king now, and had dropped the mask he wore when she had first appeared. All the gay brightness was gone from his face, and a look of terrible agony rested there instead. Then she turned once more to the king.

"O my lord!" she said, kneeling again, "such

honor cannot be for thy servant. To the queen alone belongs the king's love. Let me, I pray, be but his handmaiden, singing such songs as I may for his pleasure."

The king looked slightly displeased.

"Nay, Lydia," he said, "Persian kings have many wives, an they will. You shall be mine — my wife — my best beloved, and" — he laid his hand caressingly on her arm — "your beauty so charms me with its spell — I say to you what never Persian king has said to maid: —

"'Set me as a seal upon thy heart, beloved, as a seal upon thy arm.'"

The voice of the king was soft and low as he bent forward, and his breath swept the girl's cheek. As she felt it she sprang to her feet.

"O my king!" she cried, wringing her hands, "such love as you ask for was mine to bestow, but it is mine no longer. Lo, I have given it to another. The casket is empty! The jewel is gone!"

Artaxerxes rose from his chair, and his angry glance swept the little group.

"Let me but find the thief!" he cried, "and find him I will, and if he had ten thousand lives, they should not be enough to pay the debt he owes me!

But thou, girl, thou shalt not live to tantalize me with thy beauty and thy songs. Adna, Eros, throw her from the parapet!"

"I will not," Adna murmured to Nehe, turning pale with horror, but with a terrible look of determination on his face, and his hands sank by his sides. Lydia saw the look and action, and guessed his words. She knew it meant certain death to her lover as well as to herself if the king saw him. She must hold Artaxerxes' attention. Turning, she sprang lightly on the high parapet and faced the group.

"Thou canst not find him who holds my love, O king!" she cried, "for he knows not the jewel that is his."

Her white veil floated around her like a mist in the moonlight, but she had thrown it back from her face, and her lovely eyes looked straight into Adna's as she stood poised there on the parapet's edge. Then her clear voice rose in an ecstasy of song: —

"'I am my beloved's, and my beloved is mine,'"

she sang;—

"'Many waters cannot quench love, neither can the floods drown it.'"

There was a flutter of white garments, a gleam of golden hair, and then, as they looked, the maid was gone, and the splash in the waters far below came faintly up to the group.

"There," said the king, discontentedly, "never saw I such a maid as this. If you can find her body, Nehe, let it be laid among my own women. I may, perhaps, meet her in the realms of the blessed. May Serosh guide her feet along the bridge of judgment."

"Go, Adna, and search for her," Nehe said, turning a pitying glance on his armor-bearer; "and bury her as the king has said."

An instant later, a white-faced youth, with wide-open, horrified eyes, rushed down the palace stairs. Soon he was lifting from the water, in his strong, tender arms, a little limp body. Kissing the sightless eyes, he murmured: —

"Oh, Lydia, beloved, never will I lay you among the king's women! To-night you shall rest in my own mother's bed, and to-morrow evening I will hide you in the kindly earth, beside my father's kindred."

And he strode away in the darkness, tenderly carrying his lovely burden.

CHAPTER XV

DURING the forty days that followed the fête day Nehe had quietly sent Hanani with letters of introduction to all the Hebrews in the city and surrounding country, beseeching them to join him in fasting and prayer, that the Lord God would favor the petition he was about to make of the king.

Thus it came to pass that every morning, noon, and night, prayers went up to heaven from the houses built of sun-dried bricks, as well as from the marble rooms of the king's palace, that God would cause Nehe to find favor in the eyes of his indulgent but haughty and terrible master, and receive strength to present his petition that the Hebrews be allowed to rebuild the walls of Jerusalem.

In the meantime Hanani had been quietly making preparations for the journey, aided by the Hebrews without the palace, in order to avoid delay; for Nehe had shrewdly said that the sooner they started after obtaining permission to go, the easier it would be.

In Hanani's visits among his people he was astonished to find so many of them living in comfort and even in luxury. He had expected to find nothing but poverty and unhappiness; instead he found many of them wealthy, and some occupying positions of high honor.

Nehe explained this by telling Hanani that the religion of the Persians at the time of Cyrus was a very pure one, and so like that of the Jews as to lead the king to order the rebuilding of the temple at Jerusalem. Darius, too, was in full sympathy with the Hebrew captives, and was always ready to acknowledge their God as his own. When he ordered large supplies to be given to the returning Hebrews for their temple, he explained this action by saying that when the sacred edifice should be finished, sacrifices would be offered therein to the God of heaven, and prayers would be made to the Lord, for the life of the king and of his sons.

The Babylonian language contributed to this feeling; it was so like that of the Jews that the latter easily learned it, and this had been a great advantage to them. When a Persian found himself the owner of an intelligent slave who prayed to the same God that he himself worshipped, and who also spoke his own tongue, he naturally favored him. Thus the Jews prospered, and in time found themselves owners of houses and lands, cattle and jewels, and all the things that made up wealth in Persia.

Some of the Hebrews lived in beautiful homes, set in luxuriant gardens, and as Hanani visited them he often wondered at their devotion to their fatherland — devotion that made them willing to abandon all these comforts and luxuries, and return to a country which had been desolated by conqueror after conqueror.

The morning of the fortieth day arrived all too soon, and scarcely had the first beams of the sun come dancing across the plain, gilding the distant mountain-tops, crowning them with white splendor, and then leaping down into the palm trees that waved at their feet, before Nehe awoke and went out on the wide porch upon which his room opened. As he stood there, looking over the sleeping city, across the river and then beyond, to the towering mountains, his eyes seemed to see through them, and to behold his own beautiful city, Jerusalem the Golden, in all her ancient grandeur. Then he thought of it as it was now, desolate and broken down, and his face clouded and his eyes filled with tears.

Quickly brushing them away, he knelt reverently, and keeping his face turned toward the mountains, he lifted his clasped hands and prayed.

The morning sun shone on his pure white linen robe, until it glistened with almost unearthly splendor, and as he flung back his clustering curls and raised his dark eyes to heaven, a look came into his beautiful, boyish face, that might have been seen on that of an angel, so pure, so intense, was its sweetness and sorrow.

Just then Hanani and the Lady Sarai came out upon the porch, and seeing Nehe, they crossed over to him, and knelt silently beside him, as, without apparently noticing them, Nehe began that impassioned prayer that has come ringing down the ages: —

"I beseech thee, O Lord God of heaven, the great and terrible God, that keepeth covenant and mercy for them that love him, and observe his commandments, let thine ear now be attentive, and open thine eyes that thou mayest hear the prayer of thy servant. Remember, I beseech thee, the word that thou commandedst thy servant Moses, saying, 'If ye transgress, I will scatter you abroad among the nations; but,'" and here Nehe's voice lost its mournful cadence and rose clear and joyous, "'but if ye turn unto me and keep my commandments and do them, though there were of you cast out into the uttermost part of the heaven, yet will I gather them from thence, and will bring them into the place that I have chosen to set my name there.'

"Now these are thy servants and thy people,

whom thou hast redeemed by thy great power, and
by thy strong hand."

Then the memory of what he must do that very
day came flooding over him, and his voice grew even
more soft and sweet as the pleading prayer went
on: —

"O Lord, I beseech thee, let now thine ear be
attentive to the prayer of thy servant, and to the
prayer of thy servants who desire to fear thy name;
and prosper, I pray thee, thy servant this day, and
grant him mercy in the sight of the king."

The tears were falling fast from the Lady Sarai's
eyes as Nehe finished his prayer, but she bravely
forced them back, and smiled as she laid her hand on
his curls and softly murmured: —

"May the God of our fathers go with you! May
He protect, and guide, and bring you back to me this
day in safety!"

And she bent her head and softly kissed his forehead, well knowing that another morning's sun
might never shine upon it; for fear of treachery was
ever present with Persian kings, souring the sweetest
natures, and rendering the kindest sovereigns fierce
and unreasonable, if once their suspicions were
aroused.

As Lady Sarai finished speaking, the three turned

and entered the room, and Bani came running to meet them. His grandmother stooped to kiss the child, and then she glanced around the apartment, and said sadly: —

"It was just by that pillar my poor Lydia stood the night she gave Adna the rose. Do you remember it, Nehe?"

"Indeed, I do, mother," Nehe answered. "Poor Lydia! Even yet I cannot think of her as dead."

"Lydia not dead," declared Bani, eagerly. "Lydia a boy now."

"Oh, yes, she is dead," Nehe said; but Adna, who was standing near, advanced a step with a startled look on his white face, and glanced anxiously at the child.

"Why do you say Lydia is not dead, Bani?" asked Hanani, lifting him in his arms.

"'Tause I saw Lydia," the child persisted, "and she a boy now. Adna knows," the little fellow insisted, turning to the armor-bearer, who stood near Nehe.

"What means Bani?" Nehe asked, looking keenly at Adna.

"My lord," Adna answered, "when we were in the Jews' quarters yesterday, Bani saw a young man who spoke kindly to him, and he immediately called him Lydia, fancying, I suppose, that their faces were alike."

Nehe looked at Bani anxiously. "My child," he said, "say no such word again. Should the maid come to life as a man, my life, as well as my armor-bearer's, could scarcely satisfy the king. Adna," he added sternly, turning to that young man, "you swore to me that the men found not Lydia's dead body when they dragged the river."

"They found it not, my lord," the armor-bearer answered steadily, but with a face of deadly whiteness. "My lord, I swore true."

CHAPTER XVI

NEHE was very glad, when he entered the king's private apartment that morning, to find that Artaxerxes intended to receive his friends there instead of in the throne room; for Queen Damaspia, on learning that Megabyzus, the conqueror of Egypt, was to be at the court soon, had begged the boon of hearing the story of his conquest as told by himself.

Damaspia was already seated by Artaxerxes when Nehe entered, and although the young cup-bearer had not seen her face for years, he well knew her graceful, veiled figure, and he felt that her kindly eyes were upon him, as he advanced and knelt before the king.

If Nehe could have pierced through the folds of the queen's filmy veil, he would have seen a puzzled look come into Damaspia's face as her eyes rested on the cup-bearer.

"Surely," she was saying to herself, "this is Nehe, the king's favorite; but what has changed him so?"

The air of boyish gayety that had sat on his handsome face, when she last saw him, was gone, and

instead there was come an expression of manly grav-
ity. His lips had lost the slightly haughty curve they
had worn, and had grown straight and firm, and the
smile that came into his face, as he turned to his
master, was so tender and sweet, Damaspia did not
wonder that the king's eyes also dwelt long and kindly
on his favorite.

The queen did not have time to observe him long,
however; for scarcely had the cup-bearer knelt before
the monarch, when again the curtains were held aside,
and the chamberlain entered, leading by the hand
Megabyzus, the victorious Persian general.

This renowned warrior was a large, middle-aged
man, with a stern face and keen eyes. He wore a
high, fluted cap and a Median robe of crimson wool
embroidered with crouching lions. The sleeves of the
garment were so long that they entirely covered his
hands. Beneath this robe he wore tight-fitting trousers, and his feet were encased in soft shoes. A huge
collar of gold circled his neck.

The general was unarmed, save with the short
dagger that was stuck in his belt. He advanced to
the throne and prostrated himself, as the king raised
his golden sceptre and pointed it toward him.

"Rise, Megabyzus," Artaxerxes said, graciously,
"and tell us of your achievements. Many and

various are the reports that have reached us, of how you overcame the wily Egyptians and the valiant Greeks, but we would hear the tale from your own lips."

Megabyzus rose and stood humbly enough, with folded hands and bowed head, when he began his narration; but as he went on, his form grew more upright and his eyes flashed, until the waiting courtiers could readily recognize, in the seemingly quiet civilian who stood before them, the courageous general who so often had led the Persian arms to victory.

As he detailed, one after another, the thrilling incidents of the war, the king became more and more deeply interested, and the narrator more and more graphic, until even Queen Damaspia bent forward breathlessly to listen. He told how the Grecian ships had come to the aid of the revolting Egyptians.

"They sailed up the Nile," he said, "and defeated our squadron, and besieged and took Memphis; but this was before I and my army, five hundred thousand strong, arrived."

Then he related the operations which resulted in the recapture of that town by the Persians, and told of the trouble they had when the Greek fleet fled to the tract called Prosopitis, which was a portion of the

Delta, completely surrounded by two branch streams of the Nile. Here the fleet was besieged for eighteen months, until Megabyzus contrived to turn the water from one of the two streams, leaving the Greek ships exposed to their attack. It was an easy matter then for any army of half a million men to surround and conquer the Greeks, being a remarkable instance of the capture of a fleet by an army.

"It was a wise and brave deed," the king said, when Megabyzus had finished this portion of his recital, "and wisely and bravely done. Was it not, my friends?"

And Artaxerxes looked around upon the seven princes, who came forward and congratulated Megabyzus most heartily on his exploit.

Nehe's heart sank as he listened to the rejoicing around him. How could he present his own private griefs on a day like this? This morning the king would expect all his household to rejoice with him, and he would have no inclination to redress private wrongs. Nehe told himself that he must await a more favorable opportunity to prefer his petition.

But then came another thought, one that sent all doubts and fears flying from his mind. This was not his own business. It was a weighty matter pertaining to the affairs of the Lord Jehovah. Nehe was but the ambassador of the King, and no longer could he delay his Sovereign's business.

All fear for himself and all anxiety had gone now, and nothing remained but a calm and steadfast determination to plead for his people. What was his life — what was any life — in comparison with the importance of the work committed to his care?

As these thoughts passed through Nehe's mind, the king turned his eyes upon him and sat a moment quietly regarding him. The same change in his favorite's face that had perplexed the queen puzzled the king, and he tried to solve the riddle. Something was changing his gay, boyish cup-bearer into an earnest-faced man, and nevertheless he saw, as did the queen, that there was no treachery, no deceit, in Nehe's beautiful eyes as they met his.

Then a terrible thought came into the mind of Artaxerxes.

Could it be, he asked himself, that here was the lover of the dead maid, Lydia? And the king remembered again, with sudden distrust and suspicion, that in spite of all the efforts to find Lydia's body, it had not been discovered. Could it be that Nehe had found the body and had hidden it from him?

If he had, he should die! Though he were his own son, the king would be avenged!

Then, leaning forward and fixing his eyes, now terrible with distrust and anger, on Nehe, he said, in a voice that caused every courtier in the room to turn and look at the favorite as though a bolt of lightning had fallen upon him from a clear sky: —

"Nehe, are you he whom Lydia loved?"

The cup-bearer lifted his serene eyes to the monarch's face.

"No, King Artaxerxes," he answered. "The maiden bore no love to me. Hebrews, my lord king, marry none save those of their own nation. I loved not Lydia."

Nehe's words were few, but there was something about his calm and steadfast look that instantly killed the king's suspicion; but his curiosity remained, and he asked: —

"Why is your countenance sad, Nehe, seeing you are not sick? This is nothing else but sorrow of heart."

A wave of terrible fear swept over Nehe, and for a moment he was dumb. The queen bent her gaze inquiringly upon his face as he hesitated, pale and trembling, and it seemed to Nehe as if he read sympathy in her very attitude. Then he summoned all his courage and answered: —

"Let the king live forever. Why should not my

countenance be sad, when Jerusalem, the place of my fathers' sepulchres, lieth waste, and the gates even are consumed with fire?"

The passionate pleading of his favorite's voice, and his brave, sorrowful face, touched King Artaxerxes' heart, and he answered kindly: —

"Well, for what then do you make request?"

A wave of intense gladness swept over Nehe at the kindly interest expressed even more in the king's tone than in his words, and his eyes shone with joy as he raised them to the monarch, and answered quietly: —

"If it please the king, that you would send me to Judah, unto the city of my fathers' sepulchres, that I may build its walls and save the temple of Jehovah, now being destroyed."

"Your request is a just and right one, Nehe," Artaxerxes answered, "for this is indeed a serious charge. We do not forget that Jehovah, the God of the Hebrews, hath often in times past manifested his power even here in Persia. Is it not true, Nehe?"

"True indeed, my king, and Cyrus, your own great predecessor, ordered his worship to be continued in Jerusalem; but, alas, the very priests at his altars are carried prisoners by the fierce Samaritans. I would go to save my city and the Lord's temple."

"Your request is granted," Artaxerxes said after a

moment's consideration, "for the Lord Jehovah is
a powerful God. I would not wish to incur his displeasure."

Hereupon the queen leaned over and whispered
something to her husband, and the monarch resumed: —

"I know that so loyal a subject as you, Nehe, may
be trusted not to foment rebellion in my far-away
province; but if your petition be granted, for how
long will your journey be, and when will you return?"

"Only so long, O king," Nehe answered, "as it
may require to build the walls and strengthen the
gates. Then I will surely return."

"I shall miss you," the king added, "but you have
my royal permission to go. What provision have you
made for your journey?"

"Little as yet," Nehe replied, "for I had not my
lord's permission. But, if it please the king, let
letters be given me to the governors beyond the river,
that they may convey me over till I come into Judah;
and then, as I shall need wood in the building, grant
that I may have letters to Asaph, the keeper of the
king's forest, instructing him to give me beams for
what I shall require."

The king smiled graciously.

"All you ask for, Nehe," he said, "is yours; and,

besides, you shall have captains and soldiers to protect you in your perilous journey, from the fierce tribes of Arabs that roam over the desert. And now, Hatach," turning to the haughty nobleman who stood near, "what of the lion hunt? Have you arranged it to your satisfaction? By the way, send the page Berces for Harbana. I would consult him also about the arrangements."

Hatach looked uneasily at the king, and then hesitatingly answered: —

"O king, knowest thou not that Queen Amestris demanded at daybreak the twelve pages of the court whom she won at dice from you last night, and that the page Berces was among them?"

"Yes," the king replied, "so she did, but I will send at once and order the return of Berces. He is the handsomest page of my train, and I like also his cheerful spirit. Yes, the queen mother shall return him. I bargained not to give her my choicest youths. She must be content with others. Go at once, Hatach, and bring him back."

Hatach prostrated himself at the monarch's feet.

"O king," he cried, "punish not thy servant that thy command cannot be obeyed. The page Berces is no more. The Queen Amestris ordered the youths to be buried alive an hour ago, an offering to Pluto, the god whom she worships."

CHAPTER XVII

THE caravan of Lord Nehe had for three days been travelling on its way to Jerusalem over the famous post road built by King Darius. As evening fell on the third day, they encamped by one of the many irrigating canals leading out from the river Euphrates, which they had just crossed.

The camp from a little distance looked as if an army might be resting there. Tents were springing up in every direction, and among them bright fires were gleaming, around which were gathered busy men preparing their evening meal. The musical calls of the camel-drivers could be heard, soothing their animals, as they unloaded and fed them for the night. Older sisters were hushing babies to sleep, while the mothers busied themselves about the tents; for when it had become known throughout Susiana that Lord Nehe was returning to rebuild the city of Jerusalem, a large number of patriotic Jews availed themselves of the permission of King Artaxerxes, gathered their families, and went with him.

Laughter and songs came from that portion of the camp where the soldiers were gathered, as they unharnessed their horses and prepared for the evening rest. In front of one of the larger tents Lady Sarai sat, with her sons and little Bani. They were a very cheerful family party as they watched the preparations of their servants for the supper.

"We have made good progress, have we not?" Lady Sarai said, addressing Nehe. "If we continue to journey as rapidly, we ought soon to reach Jerusalem."

"Oh, yes, mother," Nehe answered. "One would scarcely think that so large a caravan as ours could journey so rapidly and safely."

"I think," said Hanani, joining the conversation, "the Lord God has been with us, although we have soldiers to protect us. How kind it was in the king to provide us with so large a guard for our journey."

"Yes," added Lady Sarai, turning to Nehe; "do you not remember hearing how Ezra, when he led his band of Hebrews back to Jerusalem, stopped here, and for three days the whole caravan prayed for God's protection in crossing the dangerous lands that lay between them and Palestine?"

"Had they no guard at all, mother?" Hanani asked.

"None," Lady Sarai answered; "for Ezra said that he was ashamed to require of the king a band of soldiers and horsemen to help him against the enemy in the way."

"I don't see why," Hanani said.

"Because," she answered, "Ezra had spoken unto the king, saying, 'The hand of our God is upon all them for good that seek him, but his power and his wrath are against all them that forsake him.'"

"What a wonderful journey Ezra's was!" said Nehe, thoughtfully. "God surely led all those thousands of helpless men, women, and children through this dangerous and unknown land, in safety to Palestine."

"I pray that He may do as much for us," Lady Sarai added; "for after all, of what avail is human aid against the terrible floods of these plains and mountains or the simoom of the desert?"

"One of your dangers, at least, you need not dread, lady mother," Nehe interposed. "We shall not cross the desert at all. The post road does but skirt it. Nevertheless, I do pray for the protection of the Lord God."

"How great is your faith in prayer, mother!" Hanani said. "Jerusalem is full of sad memories to me. Pray God to restore my Hannah and Jamin!"

"Do you pray yourself, Hanani?" Lady Sarai asked, softly.

"Pray!" Hanani exclaimed, eagerly. "My life is just one prayer. At first I was stunned. All I could do was to bear. But now, day and night, I beseech the Lord God to give them back to me. Oh, mother!" he continued, vehemently, "if you only could see them! Hannah, with her eyes like a doe's — dark, soft, and beautiful, and her hair, curling in little waves from her forehead, and with sometimes an escaping lock turned back in a soft curl as if it were loth to leave so sweet a face! And Jamin! How strong and straight and brave he was, ever ready for a frolic, but a boy to be trusted as one trusts his brother."

Lady Sarai glanced pityingly at him.

"My son," she said, "I know all your sorrow, and I believe that you will one day know all the joy I feel when I look at you. Take courage! Already great good has come from your grief, and more shall surely follow."

"I think you are right, mother," Nehe said. "Brother, let us look forward with hope. Every day brings us nearer the land where your loved ones live."

"True," Hanani assented. "What a comfort you

two are! Where does our road lead us to-morrow, brother?"

"We shall follow the river north, skirting the desert all day," Nehe replied, "following the same route that you took, Hanani, when you came to Susa."

"Then we shall pass directly by the old city of Nippur," Hanani said. "The caravan leader told me many curious stories of it as we passed on our way before."

"Nippur?" repeated Nehe, interrogatively; "Nippur? What do I know about Nippur, mother?" And he turned with a smile to the Lady Sarai.

"If you remember what your father taught you when you were a boy," she answered, "you know that it was there that the first inhabitants of this country endeavored to build the Tower of Babel."

"Yes," Hanani interposed, "and our guide told me, as we passed, that even yet remains of the ancient tower may be seen."

"I know," said Nehe, "and there is a tradition at the court of Susa, that, deep down under the Temple of Bel, lies a magnificent library, telling of the doings of Babylonian kings dead and gone these thousand years.

"How I wish we had time to stop and examine it!" Hanani exclaimed.

"I am afraid that you would have to dig down twenty or twenty-five cubits to find it," Nehe added; "for the dust of centuries covers it, if it is there at all, for we have only the word of tradition that it is. The city itself was in ruins when our father Abraham started for the promised land."

Hanani looked reverently around him.

"How strange it is," he said. "When I set out to Susa, it seemed as if I were going to an utterly foreign country, but now that I am here, where so many of our people have preceded me, it seems as if I were visiting the home of my fathers."

"And so you are," Lady Sarai answered. "It was from this very plain that our father Abraham came, and his eyes must have rested, as ours rest now, on its long, level stretches, with the river flowing through."

"We would not have to go back very many years," Nehe said, "to find another wonderful event in Jewish history, for it was here, on the banks of this very canal, leading away from the river Euphrates, that Ezekiel saw his wonderful vision."

Hanani leaned forward eagerly.

"Is it true," he asked, "that this canal is the river Chebar?"

"Yes," Nehe replied, reverently, "and the land

about here has always seemed to me holy ground. It may be that Ezekiel rested just as we are resting, on the night God spoke to him, beneath these very palm trees."

There was silence for a moment, and then Hanani turned to Nehe with the remark: —

"You said that Nippur was in ruins when Abraham set out for the promised land, but it seemed to be a fairly prosperous city when our caravan passed it two months ago."

"Oh, yes," Nehe replied, "Nippur is in very good order now. See, I have here a bill received only to-day from the merchant Asshur-Bel Didu, for dates which he is to furnish our caravan. I shall forward the bill to the king to-morrow, by the slave Satzo. Perhaps you would like to see the Babylonian writing," he continued, drawing a small, sun-dried brick from a wallet that hung at his side, and handing it to Hanani.

"How curious," Hanani said, examining it. "The Babylonians evidently intend that their writings shall last forever."

"It is well that something of theirs should be everlasting," Nehe replied, restoring the brick with its writing, which was a series of curiously indented marks, to his wallet, "for their cities certainly are not; and that leads us back to where we started. The city of Nippur, for example, has been building and rebuilding for the past three thousand years. Every time the city is destroyed by its foes, when the inhabitants recover themselves they build a pavement over the old ruins and start a fresh city."

"Is that what raises it so high from the plain?" Hanani asked.

"Yes," Nehe replied. "I have no doubt it was quite a mound when Abraham passed by on his way to Canaan. He must have looked with curiosity at its walls, thirty-five feet thick, within which the ruined Tower of Babel was still plainly visible."

"His was another wonderful journey over this same road," Hanani said. "How many times God has led His people through this strange land!"

"If the hand of our God be with us as it has been with those who have gone before us," Nehe said, reverently, "we shall be in Jerusalem within thirty days. Oh, mother!" he cried, rising and turning toward her eagerly, "I can scarcely realize that in a month I may see the city of David, and then make it once again the pride and hope of our nation."

"I thank God," Lady Sarai said, clasping Nehe's hand, "that such honor may be given to my son."

Just here Adna joined the little group, his face, once so bright, wearing its usual look of quiet sadness. As he bowed respectfully to Lady Sarai, Nehe turned to him and said: —

"Adna, how come that young camel-driver, Ariel they call him, to be engaged? I questioned the overseer of the camels, and he said you had done it."

"My lord," Adna replied, "he is a young lad in whom my mother takes a deep interest — so deep, indeed, that she made me swear to her, upon my faith and honor, that I would guard and protect him on the journey, and deliver him, when we reached Jerusalem, into the hands of a friend."

"Who is the friend?" Nehe asked.

Adna looked troubled.

"My lord," he said, "I know not. My mother wrote the name on a piece of parchment, and gave it to me in a sealed cylinder, which she told me not to open until I reached Jerusalem."

And he took out a tiny roll from his pocket and handed it to Nehe.

"I like not the look of it," Nehe said, regarding the roll closely. "The lad is no camel-driver. That is evident. Had you not helped him these last two days, I doubt if he could even have kept up with the caravan. I think I shall send him back to-morrow to Susa, with a guard that goes to report to the king our safe passage of the river."

"Oh, my lord, I pray you let him continue on the journey!" said Adna, eagerly. "He is so kindly, so gentle. He has been the greatest comfort to me in my sorrow. He is a good lad, my lord. Will you not let him go on?"

"No, no," Nehe answered, decidedly. "He shall return with the guard. I fear me he is running away from the king's displeasure, and it ill behooves me, Adna, to be a party to any treason against the monarch."

"I fear the same, brother," Hanani said. "I noticed the lad to-day, and, believe me, he is gentle-born. Those shapely hands of his never held a goad before. And when one of the drivers struck him this morning, he shrank away and cried out, almost as a girl might have done. I think you are quite right in sending him back to Susa."

"Oh, my lady," Adna cried, turning with a pitiful look of appeal on his face to Lady Sarai, "will you not see Ariel? I feel sure that he has done no wicked thing against the king."

"Wicked or not, he must go back to-morrow," said Nehe, decidedly.

"My son," said Lady Sarai, turning to him, "open

the cylinder. Perhaps it may explain some of the mystery concerning the boy."

Nehe broke the wax and drew out the tiny roll of parchment, on which was written, in Hebrew characters, these words: —

"For the honor of womanhood, will not Lady Sarai, mother of Lord Nehe, take under her care and protection the lad Ariel?"

As Nehe read these words, the little group looked into each other's faces with astonishment.

"I will see the boy at once," Lady Sarai said, turning to Adna. "If he is going back to-morrow, there is all the more need for me to understand the mystery to-night. Adna, take me to him."

Adna turned and led the way through the camp, until they reached its outskirts, and then advanced to a little clump of bushes. Here he motioned to Lady Sarai to stop while he went forward a few steps. The night was fast descending, but enough light still remained to show Lady Sarai that Adna stopped beside a slight boyish figure, clothed in the garments of a camel-driver, lying stretched on the grass.

The lad was breathing heavily, as if utterly exhausted, and occasionally a faint moan escaped through his closed lips. He started up with a frightened cry as Adna bent over him, but when he saw who it was that roused him, he sank back on the grass and cried: —

"Oh, Adna!"

And at the sound of his voice Lady Sarai took a quick step forward, with a startled look on her face, while the boy, not seeing her, went on: —

"I am so tired, so tired! I ran as hard as I could all day, but the camels go so fast! I am afraid of them, too. Their great long legs are so strong. And one of them bit at me to-day, with his cruel white teeth. I am so afraid of the camels, Adna!"

"Never mind, Ariel," Adna said soothingly. "Perhaps you would like to go back to Susa. Lord Nehe says you may return with the guard to-morrow."

The boy sprang to his feet with a cry of utter despair.

"Oh, Adna," he exclaimed, "I cannot go back! I cannot! Though I die on the way, I must go forward to Jerusalem!"

And then, before Adna could catch him, the lad sank fainting to the ground. Lady Sarai stepped quickly forward and knelt over the prostrate boy.

"Run, Adna, and get me some water," she said, "while I undo this heavy leathern coat."

As Adna turned to run for the water, Lady Sarai unfastened the garment, and there saw to her astonishment, beneath a face and neck brown as the brownest Arab's, a breast of snowy whiteness, on which blazed a jewel that she remembered seeing many a time about her lost Lydia's pretty dimpled throat. It was a keepsake the dead girl had valued more than all her other possessions, because it was one which she wore when she was stolen from home.

A few moments later, when Adna returned, he stopped in amazement at the sight which greeted him. Lady Sarai was holding the boy's closely cropped black head up against her breast, with a look of wonderful happiness on her usually serene face, while the boy, with both hands clasped in hers, was murmuring: —

"He heard my prayer, Lady Sarai, and delivered me out of the power of the king."

As Adna advanced with the water, Lady Sarai looked up and said: —

"Go and order one of the extra litters sent here, Adna. The lad is sick. But your mother was right in committing him to my care. I will guard him, and he shall journey to Jerusalem with us."

Deeply wondering, but greatly relieved from his burden of anxiety, Adna turned away.

CHAPTER XVIII

O N an oasis in the desert of Moab, one pleasant morning in the early autumn, a beautiful Jewish woman sat in a large tent, busily at work weaving. As she worked she occasionally lifted her sorrowful brown eyes, and glanced through the camel's hair curtains that were looped back from the entrance of the tent to admit the light and air.

The tent itself was a large one, as befitted its importance, for it was the home of the great Bedouin sheik Imbrim. Around it at irregular intervals were grouped the tents of others of his tribe. Numbers of thick, broad-tailed sheep were grazing near, and bare-limbed, black-eyed children raced in and out, or, moving more sedately, carried earthen pots of water, well-balanced on their heads.

A large herd of camels were picketed under the palm trees, and fine, delicately formed horses, with eyes of almost human intelligence, and gracefully flowing manes and tails, moved about among the tents with the freedom of house dogs. Picturesquely dressed men, whose loose robes gleamed whitely in the morning sunshine, were seated in front of the tents in close conversation, or, with eager, animated haste, were passing to and fro.

The oasis was one of those fertile spots that lie in the midst of the wild and desolate wastes of the Arabian desert. For miles around stretched the burning sand, but far across it could be seen Mount Nebo, raising its lofty head into the clouds.

The woman who was weaving found it hard to interest herself in her labor that morning, although the beautiful carpet upon which she was at work might well have claimed her closest attention. But there was an atmosphere of stir and bustle about the camp that disturbed her. When Sheik Imbrim sat with some of his most trusted men clustered close about him, as they were sitting now, she knew that they were planning a marauding expedition against some one. Some home would be rifled, or some helpless caravan would be fallen upon, and those who were with it killed, or led captive as she had been. She knew by the way in which the men were catching and saddling the horses that the start would soon be made. The women were beginning to bring out of the tents long, cruel lances, and bows and arrows, for their husbands.

As she watched these preparations for an attack,

a sturdy, handsome boy entered the tent, and she held out her hands eagerly, saying: —

"Oh, Jamin, my son, have you come?"

"Yes, mother," the boy answered. Then approaching nearer to her, he put his arm around her neck and drew her face close to him as he whispered: —

"Mother, Sheik Imbrim says I am to go out with the tribe to-day. Word has been brought that a rich caravan will go over the road that skirts the desert, on its way to Jerusalem. They think it will pass about mid-day to-morrow, and we are to ride to-day into the mountains and hide ourselves at the pass, where we can fall upon the caravan as it goes through. I am to be taken with other boys of the tribe, to hold the horses, in case the men should wish to leave them."

"Oh, Jamin," the woman whispered back, passionately, "it is wicked and cruel work, and I dread the dangers of the desert and of the battle. I cannot let you go!"

"Jamin!" a stern voice called, "get your horse, boy! Hannah, unloose your clasp; the boy must come!"

Hannah started with a frightened cry as her eyes fell on the dark face of Sheik Imbrim, but Jamin straightened himself as a man would have done, and looked the Arab straight in the eyes.

"Go, Jamin," his mother whispered hurriedly; "and may our God protect and guard you."

At her words, the boy turned obediently, kissed her, and followed the chief out of the tent.

Hannah would have been glad to leave her weaving and go out with the rest of the women to watch the hurried preparations the men were making, but although her work was so tedious that it required ten thousand of those small bunches of wool that she was fastening in place, following the pattern her mistress had sung to her that morning, to make a square foot of the finished carpet, she knew the practised eye of old Leah would detect any lagging if the weaving went not steadily forward, and therefore she could only watch the tribesmen as they mounted their horses and rode hurriedly away.

Although it was early in the day when the party started, the men rode hard and fast over the terrible desert, then up through the wady, until at last they reached the mountains of Abarim. Up these the party hastened, until they arrived at the narrow pass where the caravan route crosses the range and then winds down to the plains of Moab before it fords the river Jordan on its way to Jerusalem.

Sheik Imbrim carefully inspected the ground around the defile and then led his party straight up the mountain by a footpath so narrow that it took a practised eye to follow it. So rough and precipitous was this path, that it was with difficulty the horses, intelligent animals though they were, could be induced to mount it, but at last the entire party succeeded in making the ascent, and found themselves on a wide shelf of rock overlooking the long road that led to the pass.

This shelf of rock rested against the mouth of a large cavern, which evidently had been used by the Arabs before, for traces of camp-fires were to be seen about its mouth, and gourds were hung at the small spring of water that gurgled at its back.

"We can make ourselves comfortable here for the night," Sheik Imbrim said to his men. "The caravan will not be here before to-morrow at noon."

It was an easy matter for these Orientals to pass a night in the open air. The water in the cavern supplied them and their horses with drink, and Jamin was astonished to see the Arabs bring out, from some hidden recess in its depths, dates and parched corn for them all.

The men were intensely weary with their journey, and scarcely had night fallen when they wrapped themselves in their mashlahs and were soon asleep. But no sooner had the morning sun crept down the mountain side than the Arabs arose, ate their frugal breakfast, and then busied themselves caring for their horses. As Jamin mingled among them, although no one had told him, he gathered from their conversation just what their work was to be that day.

The caravan which was approaching was guarded, so the spies sent out by Sheik Imbrim reported, by a very large body of soldiers, who rode in front. After these came many camels, heavily laden, and behind them a large number of men, women, and children, riding on horses, on camels, and in litters, while a very small body of cavalry brought up the rear.

Sheik Imbrim seemed surprised and troubled at the number of soldiers that guarded the caravan, and for a time the Arabs seemed to be on the point of abandoning the proposed attack; but the sheik's son, a long-limbed, slender young Arab, with keen, fierce eyes and a voice as soft and low as a woman's, was very loth to relinquish the project.

The booty would be immense, he urged, and he had a scheme by which he thought they could capture at least a part of it. His plan was to allow the guard and part of the camels to go through the defile unchallenged. There would be a great deal of noise and confusion during the passage, on account of the narrowness of the way, and it would be an easy matter to separate part of the caravan and drive it backward. The large company of men, women, and children would make it impossible for the small rear-guard to use their weapons effectively. A few of the Arabs could guard the pass, to prevent that portion of the caravan which had gone on from returning, while the rest would stampede the camels and start them headlong down the road. This would be done so suddenly that before the soldiers could realize what was the matter, they would be overpowered in the confusion.

The plan seemed feasible, and after much excited debate it was adopted, and the rest of the morning was spent in hurried and eager preparations for the attack. Spots were chosen with care all along the path, in which men were concealed, and the most minute directions were given to each one concerning his exact work.

Jamin, with the other boys who had accompanied the expedition, were placed on a high cliff at some distance from the men, with instructions that when the fighting began, they were to roll huge stones down the mountain on the heads of the rear-guard. As the boys lay there, quivering with excitement and waiting for the approaching cavalcade, one of them whispered to Jamin: —

"Father says that such a large caravan has not passed this way since the great leader Ezra took his host to Jerusalem."

"But these are not Jews?" Jamin said, interrogatively.

"Oh, yes, they are," the boy answered. "They are all Jews, guarded by the cavalry of King Artaxerxes. But that won't keep us from attacking them. The Arabs have no king."

"Did you attack the other caravan?" Jamin asked, his heart sinking at the thought that it was his own people who were so soon to pass through the defile.

"No," the boy answered. "All the Arabs of the desert intended to, but a strange sickness fell upon our tribes at that time, and Ezra journeyed unharmed, for we were unable to fight."

"Hush you, lads!" called an older youth, warningly. "They will be coming shortly. We shall see them first around that sharp bend in the path. Listen! I can hear their sound now. Get into your places behind the stones!"

The boys hastily secreted themselves, all save Jamin. He turned and crept cautiously into the bushes, until he was hidden from sight of the others.

Then he ran toward the bend in the path. He ran as if his life and the lives of all he loved depended upon his going. One thought animated Jamin now. He must reach the bend in the road before the caravan did! He must warn the Jews of their danger!

It was hard work making his way along the hillside, for ravines and heavy boulders interrupted his progress, and he was obliged to keep himself out of sight, lest the Arabs should see him and call him back. On he plunged breathlessly, scrambling over rocks, tripping over tree-roots, gliding from one boulder to another, until at last he reached the turn and knew he was safe from observation.

Jamin was so thoroughly exhausted by his struggles, that for a few moments he lay helpless on a rock, his heart beating so hard and his breath coming so fast, that at first he feared he could not make himself heard when the caravan should reach him — and it was coming rapidly on. Far down the mountain and across the desert it stretched, a long, straggling column; and to his ears arose a very Babel of sounds — the rattling of armor, the tramp of horses, the shouts of camel-drivers, songs, laughter, crying of children — a confused murmur, all joining in a roar which Jamin feared would drown his voice.

It was not his purpose to go down into the cara-

van, even though his own people were marching
there. They might welcome him, but they would
take him to Jerusalem. And he *must* stay with his
mother. He was all she had to guard and protect
and comfort her. He must only warn the caravan
and then slip away.

As the head of the column was nearing the turn of
the mountain, the boy sprang upon a projecting rock
high above their heads, and waving a large green
branch, he called;

"My lord, my lord!"

The advance guard of the caravan did not see him,
but a handsome young man riding with its leader
touched his arm and called his attention to the boy
on the mountain side.

"My Lord Nehe," he said, respectfully, "do you
suppose yon child has a message for the caravan?"

Lord Nehe glanced up impatiently. It was no
light matter to halt at such a place, but something
in the boy's attitude and in the intense expression on
his face made him turn his horse, as he called to the
boy: —

"What is it, my lad?"

"I am a Jew," the boy shouted, "come to warn
you that the Arabs lie in wait for you at yonder pass.
Be warned, my lord, and go softly."

And, slipping from the rock, Jamin ran back into the underbrush.

He ran back even more swiftly than he had come, for he felt certain that he would be pursued; and so he was, though the soldiers sent after him soon gave up the chase and returned to Nehe, reporting that it was impossible to reach the rocky ledge at that point, and that long before they could get there the boy would be beyond their reach.

Joy and terror struggled in Jamin's heart as he ran — joy that he had warned the caravan, terror lest his absence had been discovered; but when at last he slipped around the boulder's side and crept to his place by a large rock, he was overjoyed to find that he had not been missed.

And now ensued another long period of suspense, which was inexplicable to the waiting Arabs. So long, indeed, was this period that at length Sheik Imbrim himself crept silently and swiftly to Jamin's side, for he was stationed nearest to the turn of the road. The old Arab peered down through the sheltering bushes to the path beneath and muttered: —

"It's strange that they do not come. The cavalry should have passed this way a good half-hour ago. See, the shadow of the rock has changed, and is

falling now on the other side. Why have they halted?
Why do they not press forward?"

"I think they are coming, O sheik," Jamin answered, his heart beating so fiercely that it seemed as
if his words would choke him. "See, they are turning
the bend in the road now."

"'Tis well!" exclaimed the sheik. "As soon as the
cavalry pass, I will rejoin my men. I would make
sure how many have gone through. Count them,
Jamin. Ishmael reported that a thousand mounted
men were in the guard."

Quivering with excitement, the two leaned forward
and watched the advancing column. It was composed of splendid-looking soldiers, clothed in scarlet
kilts, with breastplates and shields of shining brass,
each armed with two javelins and a bow with a quiver
of arrows, the latter slung at the back. The horses
were also protected with similar armor, so that horse
and rider shone like brass in the bright sunshine.

The men rode two abreast slowly and warily forward, until they reached the narrowest part of the
pass, and then, instead of going through, to Imbrim's
surprise and consternation, they halted, and each
faced about, making living walls of brass between
which the caravan, it was now plainly to be seen, was
to pass.

Slowly the army came on, until two solid lines of soldiers extended from one end of the defile to the other. Silent and motionless they stood, carefully scanning every rock and tree-trunk, every bush and rising hillock. No chance for a surprise was there here, no opportunity even for Sheik Imbrim to rejoin his men. Chagrined and disappointed, he could only cower beside the brave boy and gaze upon the great host as it proceeded safely through the pass. What an interesting sight it was to the boy, to see these men that he had saved, and his heart leaped with joy as he watched them march along.

Through the living lane came first a small body of horsemen, dressed in a lighter armor than those who had stationed themselves along the path, for their breastplates were only of quilted linen, with helmets of bronze, and their weapons were shining swords of the best steel, the finished productions of the workshops of Phœnicia and Greece.

In the midst of this body of mounted men came a handsome soldier, clad in a pure white linen garment, and armed only with a short sword. He was riding a spirited steed whose glossy coat was as white as the rider's own raiment. So commanding and princely was the air of this soldier, and so well and gracefully did he manage his horse, one knew instinctively that

here was the leader of the caravan, and one born to
command.

Beside him rode his armor-bearer, a youth of
scarcely more than twenty, clad from head to foot
in shining steel, and carrying his master's armor.

Following this body of troops came the long, long
line of heavily laden camels, with upraised, disdain-
ful heads, passing up the rocky steep as swiftly and
silently as shadows might.

Before the camels began to go by, the leader and
his armor-bearer had drawn to one side, and now they
stood waiting, apparently either reviewing the troops
or watching for some one. This action had puzzled
Sheik Imbrim, but it was explained when, behind the
camels, was seen advancing another and smaller body
of cavalry, whose huge shields of wicker work, closely
locked together, formed an impenetrable wall around
something which they were carefully guarding.

"The choicest of his treasures must be there,"
Imbrim said; "but we shall see what they are
guarding, for the path narrows directly below, and
they will be obliged to break their ranks. The
wealth of a kingdom has already gone by; what more
can he have?"

As though in answer to this question, the com-
mander stopped the advancing squad and began its

rearrangement, in order to enable it to go through the pass. In changing their places, the soldiers lowered their shields, and Sheik Imbrim and Jamin almost forgot their caution as they peered forward in their eagerness to see what was hidden behind them.

"Only a woman!" the sheik exclaimed, in disgust. "They are guarding just a woman and a child."

But Jamin was bending forward with wide-distended eyes, and a look of bewildered astonishment on his face. At that moment, another man rode hastily forward to speak to the leader. As he did so, he turned his upraised face toward the mountain side, and Jamin sprang to his feet.

"Oh, father, father!" he cried.

But the words were scarcely uttered before a heavy hand fell on his shoulder, and he was forced down to the ground. Panting, struggling, fighting, he lay there, straining every boyish nerve and muscle and sinew in the frantic endeavor to free himself from the cruel grasp that was slowly but effectually choking him, choking him until the light faded from his eyes. His breath stopped and he lay senseless on the ground. When he recovered consciousness, the caravan had passed, and the Arabs were busy preparing for departure, chagrined and disappointed at the result of their expedition.

CHAPTER XIX

IT was midnight, and no light fell on desert and oasis save that of the stars and of the camp-fires.

No one in the Arab camp had as yet thought of sleep, and for many hours the women had been turning anxious eyes toward the desert, looking for the return of the men who had ridden forth the day before.

At length a glad cry from one of the maidens announced that she saw a dark shadow sweeping over the desert, whereupon all the women went to the edge of the oasis to watch it.

"Draw your shawl closely around you, Hannah," one of the women said to another. "The night air is very keen, and you tremble greatly."

"It is not altogether the night air," Hannah answered. "I shall be glad when the tribe is safely back."

"They are coming very fast now," the other continued. "They will be here in a minute. But I fear that the expedition met with poor success. See there are no camels in yonder line that is galloping in."

As she spoke, the men began to arrive at the oasis,

and as each Arab flung himself from his horse, he
was met by his wife and children, who plied him with
eager, anxious questions. Hannah stood a little back
from the rest. She saw that the riders were weary,
chagrined, and disappointed, and she knew that it
would not be best to ask questions at such a time.

Presently the boyish form for which she was straining her anxious eyes came out of the star-light into
that of the camp-fires, and with a little cry of welcome
she ran to help him from his horse, for she saw that
he was almost fainting from weariness. His feet had
hardly touched the ground before he laid his head on
her shoulder, and all the fearful disappointment and
pent-up sorrow of that long, long ride burst forth in
a bitter cry: —

"Oh, mother, mother! I saw him, and he would
not look! I called to him! I cried to him, but he
would not stop! And Bani — little Bani — how
beautiful he was! Oh, mother! mother! what shall
we do?"

"Whom did you see, Jamin?" his mother demanded, taking her sobbing boy in her arms and
leading him quickly apart from the others, for she
saw that he had a revelation to make.

"My father!" Jamin answered; "I saw my father
go riding by on a beautiful horse, and little Bani was

there; and, mother, he looked just as he did a year ago, only larger and better! And I called to them, but the sheik stopped my cry. But I saved them, mother! I saved father and Bani!"

Then Jamin poured into Hannah's startled ears the story of the caravan, and for a while she wept with him, wringing her hands in anguish; but when he told her how he had warned the caravan, and saved his father and Bani, and all the rest, she dried her tears, and gazed at him proudly, saying:—

"Jamin, instead of weeping tears of sorrow, we should be singing songs of thanksgiving! How many nights have I gone to bed weeping, because I knew not what had become of your father and Bani! Now, although we know not all we would know, this is sure — Bani is happy and well cared for, and what a relief this is, no one but the Lord can know. And your father, too! You say he was well dressed and well attended? Then he is prospering, somewhere and somehow, though I cannot understand."

"It seems so strange, mother," Jamin answered; "he was not with a Jewish or Egyptian caravan, like those that sometimes cross the desert; but the men who guarded him were strange people, such as I saw once with the Persian governor, when he came to Jerusalem with a message from the king."

Hannah glanced up with a startled look in her eyes.

"Jamin," she said, "I think I understand it all. Many and many a time, as your father and I have sat in the evening on the roof of our little house, looking at the broken-down walls of Jerusalem, I have heard him say, 'O that God would raise up some messenger wise enough and strong enough to persuade Artaxerxes Longimanus to allow us to finish the work which Darius commanded us to stop!' Then he would tell how Sanballat, our great enemy, was growing old now, and he did not believe that Sanballat could influence Artaxerxes as he had influenced Darius. Who knows," Hannah exclaimed, "but that your father has gone himself to the Persian king, and has come back with the royal permission!"

"Whatever he has tried to do, mother," Jamin replied, "he has certainly succeeded; for though his face was care-worn and sad, great honor was paid him by all that were with him, for he rode up to the leader of the caravan as if they were close friends, and it was Bani that the soldiers were guarding so carefully."

"If it be as I suspect," Hannah said, "we may well spend our days in captivity, Jamin, for the glory of our nation will be restored."

"Father will not leave us in captivity," Jamin

added, proudly. "If he has horses and armies, he will come and save us."

Hannah stroked the brown head lovingly.

"Your father does not know we are here," she said. "He thinks we are with Sanballat in his strong, walled city of Samaria. He does not know that we were sold to Sheik Imbrim. But do not be disheartened, Jamin! I have not put my trust in horses and chariots, but in the God of our fathers. He will yet deliver us! Now, hearken! If it be as I think, that your father has come with the governor to rebuild the walls of Jerusalem, it will make a great disturbance among the Samaritans and these Arab tribes, and we shall soon hear of it. Broken-down Jerusalem lies a prey to all, but Jerusalem rebuilded is the watch-dog and tower of defence to the Jewish nation."

And the two joyfully returned to the tent.

To Hannah the days that succeeded the passing of the caravan were long and wearisome. All day she assisted the sheik's wife, grinding corn in the stone mortars, carrying water for the flocks, and weaving on her carpet. But to Jamin the time fled by swiftly and pleasantly enough. In the morning he went with the Arab boys and climbed the lofty palm trees to bring down dates for their food, or helped to tend the flocks. He liked to stand and watch the Arabs as they trained their camels, teaching them to kneel at the word of command, and to endure, with only little moans of protest, the heavy burdens that were strapped to their backs. But his greatest pleasure of all was in caring for Neko, a beautiful mare that belonged to the sheik.

Ordinarily Imbrim would allow no hand but his own to feed or caress his favorite steed, but in coming down the mountain side, the day they returned from the attempted attack on the caravan, the sheik had slipped on a treacherous stone, and sprained his ankle so severely that every attempt to stand since had brought on excruciating pain. He had therefore allowed Jamin the pleasure of feeding and attending the horse while he was unable to do so himself.

The friendship that had sprung up between Neko and Jamin was very deep on both sides. Arabian horses are almost human in their intelligence, and as Jamin fed and petted Neko, he fancied that the horse knew all he felt and thought, and he used to stand for hours with his arms around her neck, telling her tales of his far-away Judean home.

As the horse needed exercise, the sheik encouraged Jamin to ride her, and it was not long before the Hebrew boy rode Neko almost as well as his Arab

master, guiding her without saddle or bridle, by the
mere pressure of his legs and feet against her sides.

Jamin loved, too, the evenings on the desert, when
the stars flamed out like great torchlights in the sky;
but the oasis itself grew black and dark and chill with
the night. Then the ruddy camp-fires were lighted,
and the women began to prepare the evening meal,
using for fuel the shrubs that the boys had already
gathered.

While they were doing this, Hannah would mix and
knead the barley cake, which would then be put into
the bed of glowing coals and baked. How good it
was when it came out of its hot oven and they ate it!
Then, sitting around the same fire, as the evening
shadows lengthened, they would heap on more fuel,
while the old sheik told strange, wild stories, and the
fire-light played over their faces and cast black
shadows on the tents behind them.

One of the stories that Jamin liked best to hear was
about their great forefather Abraham, who had sent
his son Ishmael out into the desert to found a new
home and a nation for himself.

For a time Ishmael was satisfied with his life on
the desert, but when he was grown to be a man he
visited the home of his father, and there he saw flocks
and herds in green pastures, feeding beside lovely

streams. He saw Abraham's broad fields of waving grain, his olive and pomegranate and peach trees, and envy grew in his heart, causing him to complain bitterly of his own position. Then Abraham reasoned with him saying:—

"Son, it is true that you may not have fields and orchards, as your brethren have, but lo! on the desert you have found the best gift that God has ever given to man. Tell me, would you exchange the horse you are riding for any field in my possession?"

Ishmael looked into his mare's beautiful eyes, stroked her silky coat, and answered, "No." Then he went back to his desert comforted.

And when Jamin looked up to find Neko gazing over his shoulder with an expression of loving friendliness, he felt, with the Arabs, that the horse was God's best gift to man.

CHAPTER XX

IT was three weeks after the Arabs had returned from their fruitless expedition against the caravan, that an alarm was sounded in the camp one evening, for a stranger was approaching at full speed over the desert.

"He is a messenger from some tribe at peace with us," Imbrim said, after a glance at the rider in the distance. "No enemy or stranger would dare to approach us unguarded. Let preparations be immediately made to receive him with honor."

All the men on the oasis sprang upon their horses and galloped to meet the rider, uttering loud cries and brandishing their long lances and wildly swinging their shields as they rode. With their white robes streaming back in the breeze, they rushed like a hurricane toward the approaching horseman, who dashed forward to meet them in the same strange fashion.

One unused to the customs of the sons of the desert would have fancied that a desperate fight was about to take place, as the excited horses and men circled around each other, but this was only the Arabian way of greeting the new arrival with marks of respect.

Surrounding him as they rode, they conducted him to the tent of their sheik. Here he was given a bountiful meal of barley bread, dates, and milk. By this time it was growing dusk, and when the evening meal was finished, the brushwood fire was replenished and all the men of the tribe gathered in a close circle around him, the sheik in the place of honor, that the rider might tell them his errand.

As soon as the Arabs had taken their places about the visitor, the women, closely veiled, seated themselves within hearing, and how fast Hannah's heart beat as she eagerly listened to the tale the messenger told!

"I am here, O great and powerful chief," he began, bowing low to the old sheik, "from your friend and ally, Sanballat, the rich and powerful governor of Samaria. He bids me tell you that our common enemy, Jerusalem, which for many years has been despoiled of her power and has lain at our mercy, is arising from her ruins and endeavoring to regain her former position of strength and glory."

"How can this be?" asked the sheik. "When I made my last excursion against the city, she was utterly helpless, and we easily took from her people many flocks and much grain and fruit."

"True, O wise chief," said the messenger; "but

Sanballat bids me tell you that there has come a new governor to Jerusalem, with letters from the great King Artaxerxes, permitting him to rebuild the walls. He also carried letters to the keepers of the king's forests, and many men are now employed in cutting down huge beams to be used in rebuilding the gates."

"This is bad news, indeed," said the old sheik, "and the tribes of the desert, with the Midianites and the proud Samaritans, should join their forces and stop this building, as we stopped it in the reign of Darius."

"It is for this I am come," said the Arab messenger. "Sanballat has but just finished the beautiful temple to the Jewish God, in his city of Samaria, and it angers him that the Jews should attempt at this time to rebuild their own, for many Jews who were flocking to his city and his temple will now return to their own city of Jerusalem; and to meet this situation he has sent messengers to all his brethren of the desert, asking them to join with him in a combined attack against Jerusalem."

"Gladly will we add our strength to his," replied Imbrim; "I and my people. When is the day in which he desires us to set forth?"

"The time has not yet been chosen," said the messenger; "but watch yonder tallest mountain-peak.

The night before all the tribes are to start for Jerusalem, huge beacon fires will burn on its summit, a signal that on the following day Sanballat will join you before the unfinished walls of Jerusalem, ready and able to overthrow that presumptuous city."

There was much more talk between the sheik and the messenger, but Hannah, with her hands pressed against her heart, moved quietly back into the shadow of the great tent, and turned her straining eyes toward Mount Nebo. Already in imagination she saw the red beacon flaring there, calling the enemies of Jerusalem to its destruction, and she could not endure to listen as the plans were being laid.

Every night after the departure of Sanballat's messenger, many eyes on that desert oasis were turned toward the dark heights of the mountains of Moab, to see if the red beacon was yet glowing there.

For a whole week the anxious Arabs turned away disappointed, for they were eager for the expedition, certain of returning home, as they had done many times before, enriched with cattle and merchandise stolen from the hapless Jews. But one pair of eyes gleamed joyfully night after night when no beacon appeared, as Hannah realized that one more day had been given to her friends in which to strengthen the walls of Jerusalem.

But on the evening of the eighth day a cry of exultation went up from the Arab camp. Scarcely had
the shades of night fallen over the desert, when high
up the mountain glowed the red signal. At once all
was confusion and excitement on the oasis. The
women were set to baking barley loaves for the men
to carry with them; and the Arab warriors, gathering
around their camp-fires, devoted themselves to clean-
ing anew and resharpening their weapons, and to
boasting of the deeds they would soon do.

It was far in the night when Hannah crept into
the women's compartment of the tent and sank down
on her sleeping-mat close beside Jamin. Then began
a terrible battle with herself. A messenger must be
sent to warn the city of its peril. But who should go?
There were only two on the oasis who would be willing
to carry the warning, — she and Jamin, and she was
a woman, weak and helpless. To her the journey was
an attempt far beyond her strength. But was it not
such to him, too, she asked herself. How could she
send him? — her boy, her darling! It was impossible. He would be lost, he would perish of thirst on
those burning sands, and she would be his murderer.

Then the thought of his father's peril came flooding
over her. She pictured the sudden combined attack
of Sanballat, with all his army, united with the tribes

of the Arabs, and the fierce, cruel Midianites. In her mind she saw the unprotected workmen overwhelmed and the mothers with their children either slain or carried off into captivity.

She called to mind the other Hannah, who had given up her little son to the service of the Lord.

"But," moaned the poor mother, "that Hannah took Samuel herself and left him in kind hands, while I must send my son out into the terrible desert alone."

Hannah dared not waken Jamin even with caresses, for she wished him to get a long night's undisturbed rest. He would need all his strength, she knew, for that terrible journey on the morrow, if she should send him; but she bent lovingly above his curly head and felt his warm breath on her cheek.

Once he stirred uneasily in his sleep, and murmured, "Mother," and she caught him in her arms and pillowed his head on her breast, as she had done when he was a baby.

Thus the long night passed, and at last the shrill crowing of a cock told her that day would soon break, and reminded her that what she would do she must do quickly. With one last great effort she put aside her agony and fears. Jerusalem must be warned! Then, bending over her boy, she whispered: —

"Jamin, Jamin, my son!"

The boy stirred, and she caught his hand in hers with a clasp that they had often used since their captivity, as a warning of danger and a signal for silence. The firm touch instantly awakened him, and he sat up.

"Jamin, my boy," his mother whispered again, "rise and come with me."

As is the custom in the East, both Hannah and Jamin wore at night the same loose, flowing robe that covered them by day. As he followed his mother out, therefore, he was fully dressed.

The two were compelled to step very cautiously to avoid waking the other inmates of the large tent; and, once outside, although the darkness was intense, Hannah led Jamin swiftly to the edge of the oasis. She stopped only once, and that was for the purpose of filling her large leather water bottle with water at the well.

When they reached the edge of the oasis, they halted, and Hannah stood for a moment with her arm around Jamin, trembling. Then she controlled her emotion, and said quietly, for she realized that if he were to be successful in his strange errand she must not rob him of his courage: —

"Jamin, my boy, do you know what that red light that burned last night on the mountain side meant?"

"Yes, mother," Jamin answered. "It meant that to-morrow the Jews are to be attacked, and perhaps father will be killed. Oh, mother, how I wish I could help them!"

And in the darkness Hannah felt the boy's tears rain down on her hand that was clasped around his neck.

"No, Jamin," she said, "it meant that to-day — for the morning is close at hand — a brave boy would ride over the desert. He would ford the river Jordan just beyond the Moab mountains, and then he would dash on to Jerusalem, and cry, as he entered the gates of the city, 'Up, for your enemies be upon you!' And, my son, he will save the city and its people, his father and his brother."

"And who, mother," asked Jamin, and Hannah felt his tears cease to flow and his sturdy form straighten in the darkness, "who shall this boy be, mother?"

Hannah, lifting her pale face up to the dark sky, said: —

"Oh, Jamin, my son, it shall be you! To you God has given the honor of saving His people."

For a moment or two the boy was silent, and then, trembling with excitement, and drawing closer to her in the darkness, he asked: —

"Mother, how can I reach Jerusalem to-day?"

"Do you not remember, Jamin," she asked, "the day you went with the Arabs to attack the caravan, how you told me you remembered so well the road to the pass that leads to the Jordan, and were sure you could find it again, that some day we two might escape together?"

"Can you not go with me now, mother?" Jamin asked, eagerly.

"No," Hannah answered; "there is but one horse on the oasis that can traverse the distance between here and Jerusalem to-day — only one horse among all the Arab tribes that can outdistance all others if you should be pursued, and that is — "

"Neko," Jamin interposed. "Oh, mother, would it be right to take her?"

"Yes," Hannah replied. "Give the little bird-call that you have trained her to answer, and see if she will not come to us here."

Softly on the night air rose the "chirr-chirr" of a bird, and then Hannah and Jamin waited in breathless silence. There was no answer of approaching feet, and Hannah whispered: —

"Call again."

Again the bird-like call thrilled through the darkness, and again they listened. In a few moments they heard Neko's soft steps coming toward them, guided by the call, and with a low whinny the mare's soft muzzle was thrust into Jamin's hand.

"There," said Hannah, "God has provided you with the means of travelling, my boy; and here is your water bottle, and here are some dates and barley bread. I saved my supper for you, darling, and you must divide with Neko."

Then Hannah carefully explained all she knew of the road over which he must travel after he left the mountain pass, and bade him not to stop at the call of any one.

As Hannah stood beside Jamin in the darkness, she longed to clasp him in her arms, to kiss him with passionate fondness, and to sob out her agony on his shoulder; but again she remembered that he would need all his boyish courage and strength before the day was over, and therefore she stood beside him quietly enough, going over all the long road that lay between them and Jerusalem.

The darkness and silence were intense. There was not a sound, not even a breath of wind in the tree-tops. Then Hannah knelt on the sand and begged the help of the Lord for her boy.

"Out of my arms into Thine I put him," she said, "for all my trust is in Thee."

The heavy darkness was lightening a trifle now, and desert and sky had turned to a dark, dull gray. The winds were hushed, and there was no sound of birds in the trees, standing quiet and motionless, gray and cold as the desert itself.

It seemed to Hannah as if the world were dead, and that light could never dawn. Suddenly, as they watched, there came a faint twitter of birds in one of the tree-tops, and then an answering call. Another and another followed until the palms were full of song, and then, far out there in the darkness, a faint golden flush appeared. Was it light, or did Hannah's straining eyes only imagine it?

She pressed Jamin's hand more tightly and her heart beat more rapidly. She knew that the moment had almost arrived when the parting must come, for higher and higher swept the flush, separating the gray of the desert from the gray of the sky. Then a rosy pink came surging after the yellow. It fled along the sky until it filled the whole eastern horizon. It came toward the watchers in rolling billows of color. It reached the gray trees and painted them green, and gave to them trunks of gold and silver. It dropped down to the desert and turned its sands to amethyst and gold.

Wave after wave of color came rolling in, each

more gorgeous than the one that preceded it, and Jamin crept closer to his mother, his arms clinging to her, his questioning eyes upraised to her face. And still Hannah held him. She would not let him go until the first sunbeam should gleam across the sky. That should be God's signal to her.

Then the birds began to hush their joyous chorus. The breeze that a moment since was swaying the trees grew still. The desert listened. Something was coming. All nature grew expectant. The clouds rolled back and banked themselves as a throng of angels might, in a long, low, dark line across the horizon, leaving a pathway of gold upon which opened a gateway of pure blue. The sea of amber below smiled up at the sea of gold above. The Prince of Day was coming. He must come soon. And Hannah turned to Jamin.

"Mount, dearest," she whispered, "and, once started, do not look back. The Arabs will not miss Neko for an hour. They are to await the coming of the Midianites, and it will be nearly or quite two hours before they arrive. If you see enemies in pursuit of you, ride on the faster! Ride, but never look back!"

Jamin reached his seat on his horse's back with a light bound, and at that moment a long, quivering ray of sunlight shot across the sea of crimson and gold. A breeze sprang out of the desert, and stirred the palm trees' plumes of green. Hundreds of birds burst into an ecstasy of song; and the sun, shorn of his beams, rose out of the desert, passed through the golden gate, and marched along his appointed pathway, glorious in beauty, perfect in majesty; and Hannah knew that the moment had come when she must say farewell.

Jamin bent down to her from his height on faithful Neko's back.

"Good-by, mother," he whispered; "I shall give your love to father to-night."

"Good-by, my darling," she answered. "God be with you! Now ride for your life."

CHAPTER XXI

JAMIN leaned forward and spoke a low word in Neko's ear, at the same time touching her flanks gently with his heels. The intelligent animal gave a shake of her head, her nostrils sniffed the morning air, and with a bound she shot out into the desert; and Hannah stood alone, her hands clasped over her beating heart, her straining eyes following that little flying figure, on whose safe-going depended the fate of all she held dear.

How swiftly Jamin rode! For the first few miles it was all he could do to retain his hold on Neko's back, trained rider though he was, for the cool morning air was as bracing as wine, and nothing could have suited Neko better than a race over the desert, with the young master she loved on her back, and Hannah's soft caress as she started filling her heart with pride. Therefore she flew onward as if she knew that she was accounted the swiftest of all the horses in the desert, and was intent upon showing her speed.

The boy had so recently been roused from sleep, he thought of nothing save the task of guiding his steed in the right direction.

Soon the sun grew hot and fervid. Oh, how it blistered down on the clear, clean sand; and how the sand stretched away — miles and miles of it, blown by the wind in fantastic waves and hillocks.

And how thirsty Jamin was! Why, it was scarcely half an hour since his mother had given him and Neko water and food, and already his tongue was parched and dry. To a boy unaccustomed to the desert, this heat and thirst would have been unbearable, but Jamin cared very little for either, and the desire for water would have been harder to bear had not experience taught him that it would soon pass off.

As Jamin flew swiftly along he was overjoyed to observe, by numerous signs that greeted his eyes, that he was on the right course. He had ridden at headlong speed for an hour, and then had held Neko in, for the heat grew more and more intolerable, and, like the wise young rider that he was, he did not wish to overtax his horse at the beginning of the journey.

Another hour had gone when a sound broke the intense silence of the desert, and Jamin's heart mounted into his throat as he listened. Surely there were voices behind him! Surely there was the swift rush of horses! He turned his head for one backward look. Yes, just as he had fancied, there came a company of Arabs in full pursuit after him.

Bending low over his horse's neck, Jamin whispered in her ear: —

"Faster, Neko, faster!"

His own terrible excitement seemed to communicate itself to the horse, for with a bound she shot forward, as if until now she had but been playing at running. Now she would show what speed really was! Panting and trembling, but remembering his mother's parting admonition, Jamin held on, never once glancing back, and to his delight he saw that he had almost gained the entrance to the long wady that led to the mountain pass.

Well it was for Jamin that for ages the angry clouds had been hurling themselves in torrents against the mountain sides, and, rushing down them in fierce, headlong haste, had dashed into the desert, a mass of foaming, yellow water. But the desert had no rocks, as had the mountains, to oppose the rush of the oncoming foe, and deep ravines and valleys showed the gaping wounds the flood had cut ere it sank out of sight in the shining sands.

Jamin was very near the wady now, and he knew that its rough, uneven sides would protect him from his enemies. He had no fear of being overtaken by them. Neko was far too fleet for that. It was their arrows he dreaded, and he rode desperately, hoping they would not fire until he reached the wady; but even as the thought crossed his mind a horrid hiss struck his ear. Neko swerved to one side, and an arrow buried itself in the sand a few feet in front.

Jamin leaned closer on his horse's neck.

"Faster, faster, Neko," he panted. "It's not I alone you are saving; it's the city, God's city."

Another arrow whizzed past him, and this time so close the boy cried out in terror: —

"O God of my fathers, save me, save me!"

And as if in answer to his prayer, a rushing sound broke the stillness of the desert, a roar as of a mighty cataract, coming nearer and nearer. The Lord of the desert had surely heard the cry of his messenger; for Jamin, looking back, saw, directly between him and the Arabs, but entirely enveloping them, the dreaded simoom.

Huge columns of sand like mighty giants were whirling in a wild, fierce dance between him and his enemies, and although the air grew hazy and almost stifling with heat, he was quite out of the course of those terrible sand monsters that were enshrouding his pursuers.

"Go, Neko, go!" he shouted. "We are safe! We are safe!"

Two hours more of that swift, ceaseless gallop, and

he had ridden through the wady, crossed the mountain pass, and was coming down into the valley. How his heart beat with exultation as at last a long line of silver, running through a stretch of lovely green, told him the river Jordan lay before, and that more than half of his terrible journey was over!

It seemed as if the sight of the river filled Neko with as much joy as it did her master, for she arched her beautiful neck and neighed joyfully as she galloped up to the river's brink and then bent for a long, cool draught of that delicious water.

It was lovely there in the shade, with beautiful flowers all around them, and that wide stretch of silver water before them. Jamin almost fell from Neko's back from sheer weariness, and then he buried his face in the rippling waves.

But the river did for them what it has done for many other fainting travellers. It gave them new life, and after the two had eaten the cakes and dates Hannah had put up for them, and rested a little longer in the delicious coolness, they were quite ready to go on, though Jamin longed to linger in that lovely valley.

How beautiful it was, sweet and green and covered with exquisite wild flowers. To his boyish eyes, so long accustomed to the yellow desert sands, he thought nothing could be sweeter than the scarlet anemones that grew everywhere. And the roses! How beautiful they were, fairly begging him to pluck them. But, tempted as he was, he mounted his horse.

"It's a long way yet, Neko," he said, looking across the ford of the Jordan and up at the high mountains that towered in the distance beyond. "It's a long ride, but we shall do it, shan't we?"

And the two started bravely on the dangerous road that lay between them and Jerusalem.

While Neko resumed her steady, swift gallop forward, Jamin kept a careful lookout for any enemies they might meet on foot or on horseback. Occasionally he glanced back, but he was not much afraid of any one's overtaking him. He had traversed the road much too rapidly for that. But he kept asking himself what he should do if he were to meet a body of Samaritans coming toward him, and he finally decided that he would leave the road and try to shelter himself in the bushes until they had passed.

It was well he had chosen a plan of action before the time came when he should need one, for suddenly he saw approaching him a band of fierce, wild men, mounted on fine horses and armed with long spears and bows and arrows.

Instantly leaping from Neko's back, he led her

into the woods and then crouched down beside her, scarcely breathing, as the cruel-looking band swept past him. To his great joy they had evidently not seen him, for they kept on toward the river.

When they were out of sight, Jamin resumed his journey. He was fast approaching Jericho now, and its walls towered high before him.

All around the city lay groves of palm and sweet-scented balm trees, and fields whose perfect order showed they had very recently been carefully tended; but nowhere was any one now to be seen. Not a flock upon the hillsides, not a tiller in the fields. Even the great gates of Jericho were shut as tight as on that memorable morning when Joshua and his host encircled them.

In one way the seemingly utter desertion of the country was an aid to Jamin. No hand was there to oppose his headlong flight. But the stillness was oppressive. It augured danger in the air. Had Jamin known, the explanation was simple enough; for the energetic ruler of Jerusalem had sent to Jericho and to all the other towns in the neighborhood, and called all the able-bodied men to the holy city, to hasten the work of rebuilding its walls. The timid ones left behind had closed the gates, not knowing who might enter when the city's defenders were gone.

In spite of the time that Jamin had lost while hiding from the Samaritan band, the six miles that lay between Jericho and the Jordan were swiftly traversed, and he swept on toward the opening of the pass leading up to Jerusalem.

From time immemorial the road from Jericho to Jerusalem had been a hard and dangerous one, and Jamin's fear that trouble would meet him in the defile was only too well founded; for as Neko went thundering up the road, suddenly half a dozen horsemen sprang up from either side. They clutched his horse's bridle, and Jamin knew that he was a prisoner.

"Stab the boy and take the horse!" one said; but the other answered: —

"Not so fast! Sanballat may gain information from him. Let us take him to the king. He seems to have ridden hard and long."

"Very well," was the answer, and in a minute Jamin was being led forward through the armed crowd, until, turning a steep, sharp corner of the mountain path, he found himself in a large open space encircled by mountains and covered with men, some on horseback and some on foot; but all were well armed, and Jamin knew, without being told, that he had reached the rendezvous appointed by Sanballat. There was only one tent set up in the camp, and toward this Jamin was hastily led. Here, seated on the ground in the doorway, was an old man. He was dressed in a beautifully embroidered robe. His hair was as white as the turban which rested on it, and his snowy beard flowed down almost to his waist. His face was seamed with many marks that age and care had placed there, but his small, cunning eyes gleamed with as much fire as did those of the young warriors who were grouped around him.

In spite of his age, the venerable man wore such an air of majesty that Jamin instinctively knew that he stood in the presence of the great king of Samaria, Sanballat, the man whose cunning and power had so long kept Jerusalem at the mercy of her enemies.

The men who had captured Jamin explained where they had found him, adding that they had brought him to the king, thinking he might be able to give some information that would be of use.

When they had finished, Sanballat said briefly: —

"Show me the horse."

Neko, who had been quietly cropping the grass at some distance, was led to the king. Sanballat looked at the noble animal carefully, his eyes kindling with admiration as he noted her excellent points and her beautiful form. Then, turning to Jamin, he said sternly: —

"Boy, tell me who you are, where you came from, and where you were going with a valuable horse like that. I shall know if you lie to me."

For a moment a great wave of fear swept over Jamin, and he dared not say a word. Then he gathered his courage and answered simply: —

"My lord, I am only a boy living in the desert, but the Sheik Imbrim, my master, is good to me, and allows no hand but mine to tend his favorite horse. A week ago came messengers from the great king, Sanballat, calling on our tribe to join with other tribes in an expedition against Jerusalem. Last night the red beacon that was to assemble us flamed up and burned on the mountains of Moab, and this morning our tribe started to join Sanballat. Neko is such a swift runner that we distanced the tribe, and now I am on my way up the mountains to find my father, bearing the message that was given me. It is of great importance. Send a guard, O chieftain, and you will see my tribe approaching along the mountain passes, and let me go forward, that I may find my father, and deliver the message before Sheik Imbrim arrives."

Sanballat was so pleased to know his expected

allies were fast approaching that he did not closely
analyze the boy's story.

"Here," he said to the two warriors who had
brought him in, "the boy tells the truth. The horse
belongs to Imbrim, the Arab sheik. I know her well,
for Imbrim came some months ago, trying to sell to
me a beautiful captive Jewish woman. I refused the
woman, but told him I would buy his horse, which he
refused to part with. Let the boy mount and be off
again about his master's business, but do you go with
him. The sheik should know that the roads these
days are not safe for striplings to travel. Many a
dead body lies between here and Jerusalem, short as
the distance is. But be off with you! Guard him and
the horse well, and bring them back in safety."

Scarcely believing his ears for joy, Jamin mounted
his horse, and the three set forward on the Jerusalem
road.

For the first few miles after leaving the Samaritan
camp, Jamin was glad of the protection of the two
armed men, for they met several bands of soldiers
going down to join Sanballat's army.

On and on they went, climbing ever higher and
higher, until at last, as the shadows began to lengthen,
the soldiers grew more and more impatient, and plied
Jamin with questions which he would have found

difficult to answer, had not his boyish wit come to the rescue. He pretended not to hear or understand most of what was said to him. They were nearing Mount Olivet now, and Jamin knew that when its height was reached, the part he was playing would be no longer possible, and he wondered how he would escape, but when the time came it was easier than he could have imagined; for when at last a bend in the road led them to the other side of the hill, the soldiers checked their horses with a cry of astonishment. Two hundred feet below them, and across the valley at the foot of which ran the brook Kedron, shone the holy city, in the rays of the setting sun.

How beautiful Jerusalem was, with its palm trees and gardens, and its temple, — white, pure, and glorious, — rising tall and stately. But it was not the sight of that magnificent building, nor of the orchards and flower gardens, that called forth the cry of astonishment from the men. It was the walls of Jerusalem, the holy city. Like as the mountains are round about Jerusalem, so the walls now encircled her. No longer rubbish heaps, they rose strong and massive, and the soldiers of Sanballat gazed at them with dismay.

"By the beard of my father!" said one, "is this the wall that Tobiah said would give way if a fox were to spring upon it? Truly, we have need of all our cunning, for unless we take the city by surprise, we take it not at all."

"And by surprise we shall take it," rejoined the other. "See, among all the thousands who are at work, not one carries even so much as a sword. 'Twould be an easy matter to enter to-morrow night through yonder open gate."

"Easy enough, truly," answered the first. "But I go no farther on this search for yon lad's father. Hark ye, boy! back we go, for you have been misleading us. I don't believe you are going to your father at all."

And he reached forth his mighty hand to turn the horse.

For the last half hour Jamin had been reserving all his energies for just such a moment as had now come. Digging his bare heels into Neko's sides, he flung himself flat along the horse's back, and darted away from beneath the man's outstretched hand like an arrow from a bow.

"I do go to my father!" he shouted back; and then, lying close to the horse, he panted, "Go, Neko, go! Run, run!"

For an instant the men gazed after him, too astonished for pursuit; then, realizing what had happened, they, too, dug their heels into their horses' sides, and sped after the flying boy.

Then began a short, fierce chase. Down into the valley of Jehoshaphat they thundered, over the brook Kedron, and up the other side. How Neko ran! Her face was almost human in intelligence and beauty, as with distended nostrils and flashing eyes she tore on toward the wide-open gate of Jerusalem. How her rider clung to her, and could do nothing else but cling, panting and exhausted, as Neko flew along, excited to her best speed by the frantic cries of the soldiers behind her!

No need to urge her now, brave little rider, although she is running a fearful race, tired with her long day's journey over desert and mountain. But she has never been beaten, proud beauty that she is, and she will not be beaten now. So the three dash on toward the city.

"Send an arrow after him, Ishmael!" shouted one of the pursuers, reining up his own horse, when Jamin was within a hundred yards of the open gate. "The little traitor will escape us!"

As Ishmael fitted an arrow to the bowstring, Jamin turned on his pursuers with a cry of exultation.

"Jerusalem is saved!" he called. "I will warn the city!"

But even as he spoke the soldier drew his bow-string. The arrow sped to its mark and buried itself in the lad's shoulder. With a cry of despair Jamin sank lower on Neko's neck, as the huge gate swung to in his face.

CHAPTER XXII

A SHORT time before Jamin and the two Samaritan soldiers stood on the Mount of Olives and gazed upon Jerusalem, Lord Nehe, the ruler of the city, and his brother, Hanani, were walking toward the newly finished gate, which was to be closed for the first time that night.

As they approached the walls, Lord Nehe said: —

"How rapidly they grow! It seems scarcely possible that it is only a month since I rode this way in the moonlight, and found the wall broken and destroyed in so many places that it did not afford the least protection to the city, and every gate had been consumed by fire. I remember I turned back and entered by this very gate of the valley, and as I rode over the heaps of rubbish, in many spots there was no place for the beast that was under me to pass. You would not believe it, looking at the wall along here now, would you, Hanani? See, the valley gate is quite ready to shut. Hanun has done good work upon it. We shall have it closed at sunset to see how it works. How strong are the locks and the bolts and the bars!"

"Yes," answered Hanani, looking carefully at the splendid gate. "The cedars of Lebanon that were sent to you by the keepers of the king's forest have certainly been used with wonderful skill. I thought the gate of Uzziel, the goldsmith, would be the finest of all, but this is just as good."

The men who were at work at the gate, putting on the finishing touches, listened respectfully to Nehe's words of praise, and one of them, who seemed to be in charge, said: —

"Will you not go up on the wall, O governor? We shall shut the gate in a few minutes."

"Most gladly," replied Nehe; and then, addressing his brother, he said, "Come, let us go up, Hanani, and there we can see how Shallum comes on with his work."

They mounted the wall, where they were soon joined by Shallum, the ruler of the half part of Jerusalem, and his two beautiful daughters, Miriam and Rachel, who had come to watch their father as he directed the labor on his portion of the wall.

As Shallum stood talking to Nehe, Miriam walked to the edge of the wall and looked off toward Mount Olivet. Suddenly she turned to Hanani.

"My lord," she cried, "do you see that cloud of dust coming down the mountain toward the brook? Who do you suppose it can be that rides so fast and furiously?"

Hanani gazed earnestly in the direction in which she pointed. Then he turned to his brother.

"Nehe," he cried, "these Samaritans grow more audacious every day. See, they are chasing some one straight up to the very gates of Jerusalem!"

Nehe and Shallum hastened to join the two who were watching the race, and in the interest it excited quite forgot the closing of the gate for which they had been waiting, and for which preparations were being hastened below.

"The rider in front is only a boy!" the girl cried, turning to Hanani, as pursuers and pursued came into plainer sight. "He is only a boy, and such a little fellow at that!"

"Oh," exclaimed Nehe, excitedly, "they are going to shoot. I wish I had my bow! The wretches are going to shoot the child!"

Nearer and nearer dashed the horses, until the foremost one had almost reached them. More and more eagerly watched the little group on the wall, and a groan escaped them all as they heard the closing of the gate, and saw, by the crimson stain that appeared on the boy's robe, that the arrow had hit its mark.

"Poor little fellow!" Rachel exclaimed, as she wrung her hands in agony. "They will kill him now! See, they are dashing forward again."

But Hanani turned with parted lips.

"Nehe!" he panted, "quick! Call to them to open the gate! Quick, Nehe! The boy is my son! It is Jamin!"

Nehe rushed to the edge of the wall, and, leaning over, shouted: —

"Open the gate! Haste, haste! Open the gate!" And then the whole party fled below.

Hanani was the first to reach the ground, and just as he did so the startled men pulled back the bolts and bars, and the ponderous gate swung wide. Scarcely had it cleared the roadway when a magnificent Arab horse sprang in, and Neko and her fainting rider were safe from their enemies; for the Samaritans, after sending one or two arrows through the open gateway, hastily withdrew, knowing their prey had escaped them.

A dozen hands were outstretched to hold Neko as she stood with dilated nostrils and flashing eyes, and head tossed back as if she would say,

"See! I have won the race!" But only one pair of arms received the little form that was slipping from her back.

"Jamin, Jamin!" Hanani cried; "my son, don't you know your father?"

The boy's beautiful eyes unclosed.

"Father," he said faintly, "up! The Samaritans and Arabs be upon you in the night! Mother sent me and — her — "

But the faltering voice stopped, and the pale lids closed over the dark eyes, and Jamin lay as if dead in his father's arms.

Hanani turned to Nehe.

"Heard you that message, Nehemiah?" he cried. "It was to avert no slight danger that Hannah ventured the child's life! Do you warn and arm the city, while I carry my son to my mother."

And Hanani turned and ran hastily in the direction of the palace.

He soon reached the beautiful white marble edifice that King Solomon had built for his own royal residence, but which was now used by the governors appointed by the Persian monarch.

Pressing his little burden close to his heart, Hanani fled up the long flight of white marble steps, and crossed the porch, whose tall cedar pillars still re-

mained a monument to the friendship existing between Hiram, king of Tyre, and Solomon.

Turning to a Persian slave who stood in the doorway, he asked: —

"Where is the Lady Sarai?"

On receiving his answer, "She partakes of the evening meal, my lord," he directed his steps to the magnificent apartment that, in spite of the ravages of
the Babylonians and Persians, still held many remains of its former grandeur. Huge blocks of marble,
magnificently carved, formed a part of the wall,
while the ceiling above was painted and set with the
same beautiful, colored stones. Long, narrow tables
were placed lengthwise along the room, and were set
with gold and silver dishes, while around them, on
couches covered with silken robes, reclined the
honored members of Nehe's household, the hundred
and fifty of the Jews and rulers who daily partook of
the bounty of the young governor.

Hastily passing through this apartment, Hanani
entered a smaller one, where the ladies of Nehe's
household were gathered. This room was furnished
similarly to the larger one, and at the head table Lady
Sarai was just finishing her meal, and beside her reclined Bani. She looked up as Hanani rushed in, and
instantly went forward to meet him.

"Mother," he cried, "God has sent me back my son, but if he be living or dead, I know not. What shall I do?"

Sarai parted the blood-stained robe and put her ear over the boy's heart.

"He has only fainted, Hanani," she said. "Lay him here on this couch and sprinkle water on his face, while I stanch the blood. See," she continued, as she drew down the dusty, blood-stained robe, "the wound is but a scratch. Give him wine and water, and he will soon open his eyes."

What a joyful little group it was that gathered around the couch in Lady Sarai's room an hour later, and listened to the story Jamin told! Sarai bent over him on one side, and Hanani on the other, while Bani seemed to be everywhere at once, trying to caress his brother.

"I thought you were never coming back," he said; "I thought you had runned away!"

Over and over Hanani made Jamin repeat Hannah's last message, and then questioned him, with hungry, eager eyes, as to how she looked, and was she well, and did she talk of him?

"I will go for her to-morrow," he declared. "Not all of Sanballat's armies shall stand between me and my wife."

At last Lady Sarai drew him almost forcibly away.

"The boy must rest," she declared, "and Nehemiah needs you. He has sent word that he is working hard getting the city ready for the attack, which he expects either to-night or in the morning."

Obeying the Lady Sarai, Hanani reluctantly left Jamin quietly sleeping, and went out to the steps of the temple, where, in the light of a glorious full moon, a large concourse of people had gathered.

As Hanani joined the assembly, he saw that Nehe was about to begin speaking. His tall, graceful form stood erect and fearless in the moonlight, and his voice rang out strong and brave and clear.

The people crowded about him, listening with respectful eagerness to his words. Their shouts of applause proved how heartily they honored and respected him.

"Men and brethren," he said, "my speech shall be brief, for our time is short. The couriers who called you here told you that danger threatens. A brave young messenger brought us word to-night, at the peril of his life, that beyond the mountains of Olivet, Sanballat is gathering the enemies of Jerusalem, who hope to take us by surprise at the dawn of to-morrow. Hence, hasten every man to his home, rest until midnight, and then come, fully armed, to the walls, and we will show these heathen dogs that Jerusalem is not to be surprised."

"Is the work, then, to cease, my lord?" called a voice from the crowd.

"Nay," answered Nehe, his eyes flashing and his words ringing clear and decided. "Once we have shown our foes our strength, they will depart. After that we shall always be prepared for them. Every man must arm himself. Let those that bear burdens carry a spear. Let the men who lay the stones have each his sword girded by his side, but let half the men of every family come armed from head to foot, carrying also the bows and spears and shields of the ones at work. So shall every family defend its own members, and its own part of the wall, and our work shall not be interrupted."

"But the wall is great and large," objected another in the throng; "and if they attack us in a weak spot, what shall we do?"

"I will go constantly from one part to another," Nehe said, "and a trumpeter shall be by me; and when the enemy threatens any part of the wall, you will hear the sound of the trumpet. Then rush there, and remember, our God shall fight for us also."

Nehe added a few other directions about their arm-

ing and the place of meeting, and then dismissed the
assembly, with these last words: —

"Be ye not afraid of them! Remember the Lord,
which is great and terrible, and now go, and fight for
your brethren, your sons and your daughters, your
wives and your homes."

With a shout that reached even the startled ears of
Sanballat in his far-off camp the answer rang:—

"We will, we will!"

And the assembly broke up, to meet at midnight,
fully armed, on the half-built walls of Jerusalem.

Long before the first faint streaks of light had crept
down into the steep valleys that led up to the city,
the armies of Sanballat and his allies were advancing
swiftly but cautiously.

They hoped to take Jerusalem entirely by surprise,
for the utmost pains had been taken to keep the intended assault a secret. Indeed, so great had been
Sanballat's care, that the two men who had allowed
Jamin to escape on the night before had not dared to
return with the tale of their loss; and the king, when
they failed to come back, merely decided that they
had stolen Neko and run off with her.

Great was the surprise and chagrin, therefore, of
the crafty old king, when the first beams of golden
sunlight that gilded the huge half-built walls showed

every low and every high place crowned with glittering spears and swords.

No room was here for surprise and easy conquest. Instead of being able to rush into the city, overpowering a few laborers who might be about ready to begin work, the hosts of Sanballat found that they must face a city alive to its danger. Trumpets were sounding, banners floating, and rank on rank of those terrible spears were to be faced.

Dismayed and disheartened, the king led his armies back down the valley, and disbanded them without firing an arrow or sending a spear against Jerusalem.

"The God of the Hebrews has brought our counsel to naught," he said; "we must try to gain the city in some other way than by force of arms."

In the meantime great was the rejoicing within the walls, as the dreaded armies of Sanballat were seen in full retreat. Although the enemy was gone, Lord Nehe urged that no precautions be laid aside, and that the work go swiftly on. It was immediately resumed, and now the men worked with almost feverish impatience. No one stopped save to eat and rest. Day and night the walls rose steadily. Day and night the utmost vigilance was exercised.

"For neither I," wrote the brave and wise young ruler, in that marvellous diary of his, from which so much of this story has been taken, "nor my brethren, nor my servants, nor the men of the guard which followed me; none of us put off our clothes, saving that every one put them off for washing!"

CHAPTER XXIII

ONE clear, cool autumn morning, a week after Jamin's return to Jerusalem, Lord Nehe and Adna stepped out upon the beautiful, wide portico of the palace. Just as they were about to descend the steps, the governor remembered the specifications for a gate which he had mislaid. He sent an attendant back for them, and as the two young men stood there waiting in the early light, one who had known them in Susa could not have failed to notice the great change in them since that first night when Nehe stood in the palace garden and Adna came to join him there.

All the soft, boyish beauty was gone from Lord Nehe's face, and even the tender, wistful look that had rested there when he appealed to the king for permission to rebuild the walls of the city of his fathers had vanished, and its place had been taken by an alert, determined expression. Intense resolve and absolute fearlessness looked out from his courageous brown eyes. The very poise of his graceful form betokened strength and action, and when he spoke there was a clear, decided ring in his voice that instantly commanded the respectful attention of all who heard it. As he stood, his eyes rested alternately on the walls of the city and on its streets that were fast filling with hurrying crowds of people.

"See, Adna," he said, turning to his armor-bearer, who was gazing off toward the eastern hills, "one would scarcely know this beehive for the mole-hill it was when we came here. Do you remember how sleepy and dead it was then? A man dared hardly venture abroad before the middle of the day, not knowing what foes might lurk in its piles of rubbish. Now, to look at those crowds, it would seem that no one could be left at home. See, even the children are hurrying to the walls, carrying the arms of their fathers."

"True, my lord," Adna answered, bringing his gaze back from the hills and looking at Lord Nehe. "Your coming has made a wonderful change in Jerusalem. O my lord, if only Lydia had lived to come to this city, how safe and happy we should be!"

His voice was inexpressibly sad, and his white face showed the passionate pain that racked him.

"Safe, Adna?" Lord Nehe replied, his face softening as he glanced at his favorite, the armor-bearer. "Was Hanani's wife safe? Has my brother no burden of sorrow to carry? Had my mother none, nor the thousands of other Jews who lived in Babylon and Susa?"

"True, my lord," again answered the armor-bearer; "but peace is dawning for Jerusalem, and happiness is in store for its inhabitants, and my heart cannot forget."

"And yet," said Lord Nehe, "every day our enemies try by some fresh plot to stop the work. The wall was built so rapidly that they found it impossible to surprise us before such a thing was out of their power. Then you know how they tried to entrap me into a consultation in the Plain of Ono. But their latest scheme gives me more trouble than anything else."

"What is that, my lord?" Adna asked respectfully.

"I have just learned, through a faithful spy, that Sanballat has written a letter, to which he has obtained the signatures of the governors of all the provinces on this side of the river."

"And is the letter to your hurt, my lord?" questioned Adna.

"Why else should it be written?" Nehe asked, bitterly. "Despairing of stopping our work by force, Sanballat is trying to poison the king's mind against me by writing to him that the Jews have always been a stiff-necked and rebellious people; that once we were the proud owners of all these lands; and that if we succeed in rebuilding our city, assuredly we will rebel against Artaxerxes and repossess ourselves of our lost possessions."

"It is a cruel and unjust letter!" Adna exclaimed, vehemently.

"And yet," added Nehe, smiling slightly, "there is so much truth in its statements that I know that when the king reads it, he will command us to stop work at once. Therefore, I am pushing the building of the walls forward day and night, praying that before the order comes for us to cease building, they will be high enough to protect Jerusalem for generations to come."

"I think you will succeed, my lord," Adna added. "Surely never before rose walls as these have risen."

"Yes," said Nehe, "and I feel as if I must give them every moment of my time. So I want you to bear my greetings to the Lady Sarai. Inquire for the health of the boy Jamin, and tell of the plot which necessitates my constant presence on the wall."

So saying, Nehe strode down the marble stairs into the city, while Adna turned his steps toward the house of the women to deliver the message. This was the same beautiful edifice that Solomon had built for his favorite wife, the daughter of Pharaoh, and although the Babylonians had burned it with fire, so much remained of its marble walls and floors and porticoes that successive Persian governors had been tempted to rebuild it, so that it was once more a magnificent structure; and, to Adna's eyes, the simplicity of its pure white marble walls and floors seemed more beautiful than the gorgeous, gilded palace of the Persian king. No huge eunuch, with unsheathed sword, stood guard at the doorway of the Lady Sarai's apartments. Instead, a dainty little maiden, clad in a white garment, drew aside the curtains and softly bade him enter.

The room was simply but tastefully furnished. A few low couches, a few cushions scattered about, among which stood spinning-wheels and embroidery frames, showed that Lady Sarai looked well to the ways of her household, and, early as it was, already many maidens had seated themselves for their daily task, their bright faces and cheerful voices seeming in harmony with the lovely morning.

Lady Sarai came forward to greet Adna, and in a few words he gave her Lord Nehe's greeting and message. She thanked him graciously, and in reply to his inquiries, said that Jamin's wound was entirely healed, and that he was fast recovering his strength.

Adna bowed and turned to go, but a sudden impulse made him look back. As he did so, he caught sight of a slight girlish figure seated at a spinning-wheel in a distant corner. There was something about the graceful poise of her head and gesture of her hand as she lifted the flax, that made Adna clench his hands in sudden pain.

Then turning to Lady Sarai, he said softly: —

"My lady, ever since we reached Jerusalem, I have longed to ask you about the boy Ariel. He is safe and well, I hope?"

"Yes," Lady Sarai replied, "he is safe and well."

But the answer did not seem entirely to satisfy the young man.

"You know," he went on, "that I am to return with the escort when Lord Nehe sends it back to Susa. I had hoped to see the lad before I go, Lady Sarai. He greatly endeared himself to me in the few days I watched over him."

It was Lady Sarai's turn to hesitate, and her eyes sought the floor instead of Adna's as she answered: —

"The lad does not wish to see you, Adna. His peril was, as you suspected, very great." Her voice grew lower still. "He was, and is, a fugitive from the king. But I will bear him your message, and if he has any to return, I will give it to you."

Again Adna bowed, and turned away with a dissatisfied look. Then, catching sight of a water bottle which was standing on a table in a distant part of the room, near the maid whose form had attracted his attention, he said, courteously: —

"I am very thirsty, my lady; may I have a drink?"

And without waiting for her answer, "Yes, one of the maidens will bring it to you," he hurriedly crossed the room and poured himself a cup of water. As he did so he turned, and his eyes searched, with an eager, anxious glance, for the face of the girl whose form had aroused such a tumult of emotion within him. But the soft folds of her veil had interposed themselves between his eyes and the face he was seeking.

"Ariel," he called softly, bending toward her; "Ariel!"

The girl made a swift motion, as if about to rise; then sank back, and quietly continued her spinning.

"Ariel," he softly called again, "Ariel, my dear lad, do you know I am going back to Susa?"

The boy, if boy it was, dropped the flax and turned his head toward Adna with a startled gesture, but made no further motion, and he turned sadly away.

Retracing his steps to Lady Sarai, who was gazing at him with a startled look, he said, respectfully but sternly:—

"Was Ariel's peril so great, my lady, that he must go disguised as a girl?"

"I told you it was very great," Lady Sarai answered, softly; "and although there are no spies in my Lord Nehe's palace, until you return with the soldiers of King Artaxerxes, it will be best for Ariel not to be seen."

And Adna bowed and left the apartment.

CHAPTER XXIV

THE following morning Lord Nehe was on that part of the wall which enclosed Ophel, when he was joined by his brother Hanani. Nehe's grave eyes lighted with approval as they searched the bright, handsome face that Hanani turned toward him.

"How fast the wall goes up, Nehe," Hanani said, greeting him. "Surely you will not build it much higher. It must be forty-five cubits now, is it not?"

"Right to a cubit," Nehe answered; "forty-five high and ten wide, besides this tower which lies out, in which Palal, the son of Uzai, intends to live. I'll tell you what it is, Hanani," he continued, smiling, "I am afraid that by the time these walls are finished I shall have elevated the whole Hebrew nation, for the city is large and great and the houses are not builded, and I have had to put so large a part of the population to man the towers on the wall."

"It does seem odd," Hanani said, turning and looking toward the temple, shining white and glorious in the sunlight, "how empty the streets are of houses. What are you going to do to fill the city?"

"That is not bothering me," Nehe replied. "I

shall persuade the owners of farms and vineyards to live within the city's walls. It will be safer for them and for us. But did you hear of the strange experience I had last night?"

"No," said Hanani; "how should I?"

"True," assented Nehe; "I think that no one knows it but myself. Lean here on the parapet and I will tell it to you."

The two young men stood looking down into the King's Dale, while Adna and the trumpeter drew near, and Nehe related his experience of the night before.

"It was just after the evening meal," said the governor, "when I received a message asking me to go to Shemaiah, for he had been inquiring of the Lord for me, and had received an answer. I cannot tell you, Hanani," Lord Nehe went on, his eyes growing soft and wistful with intense feeling, "how I have longed for a message from the Lord through one of His prophets. It has been so long since He has spoken! Hence the summons from Shemaiah filled me with gladness, and I hastened to his house. On arriving there, I was ushered at once into his presence. I found an old, old man, dressed in the garments of a priest, but when I advanced and knelt for his blessing, the light in his eyes startled me. Surely never a message from the Lord Most High kindled a fire like that in a man's eye, I thought. But I waited, kneeling, for the word of my Lord.

"'My son,' he said, 'thine enemies have gained entrance to the city, disguised as laborers and farmers. The Lord has revealed to me that this night your life will be in deadly peril. Safety for you can be found only in the temple. Haste, then, my son, and hide you in the holy of holies!'"

"How did you answer him?" Hanani asked, bending eagerly forward.

"I rose up fierce and scornful," Nehe replied, his eyes kindling at the remembrance, "and I answered him, 'No, it is not my God who sent me this warning, you man of sin; but Tobiah and Sanballat, who have hired you. Should such a man as I flee? And if I were to take refuge in the temple, even to save my life, I should lose it, for no man may enter the holy of holies and live, save the high priest only, and he once a year. This you well know.' And, hot with indignation, I turned and left him."

"You answered him well, Nehe," Hanani said, sympathetically. "Now, what answer have you for me, my brother, to my request?"

"And what may your request be, Hanani?"

"What could it be," Hanani cried, vehemently,

"save this, that you give me permission to seek my wife? No one knows with what impatience I have waited for the time when Jamin should be able to lead us back to his mother."

"And he is well enough to go now?" Nehe inquired.

"Fully, I think," Hanani said; "and if you will give me but fifty of the Persian guard, I will take them and start to-morrow on my quest."

"You may have them," Nehe said, sighing a little. "You know, brother, I am expecting every day a message from Artaxerxes, commanding us to cease building the wall, and every man's labor counts; but, as you say, your journey will take you only two days. Have you a present for the sheik?"

"Yes," was the reply, "I have prepared a beautifully embroidered robe, and a drachm of gold. Mother has made ready a litter, and has laid in it garments fit for a princess. Oh, Nehe, how beautiful she will be when you see her! I can fancy her now, stepping down from her litter to greet you, clad all in white, with her eyes like stars, and her two boys clinging to her."

"Then go, my brother, and may God keep you, and bring you all back in safety."

How proud Jamin was when early next morning he

headed the little band of Persian soldiers, commanded by his father, and started on the journey to the oasis!

How his joy bubbled over! Did he know the road? Of course he knew the road! And if he didn't, Neko did! And how glad his mother would be! He pictured her in the tent, weaving, and watching the caravan approaching over the desert. He wondered if it would be possible to surprise her, but he hardly thought it would. Oh, well, it would be joy enough just to see her, no matter how they found her.

And so he talked on, and Hanani smiled sympathetically, with a joy that was deeper than any that even Jamin could feel, as the party sped forward, riding swiftly down the mountain, over the wide, shallow ford of the Jordan, then across the plain of Moab and through its mountain, and then plunged into the fierce heat of the desert.

Many times during the ride Hanani had questioned Jamin anxiously: —

"Are you sure you know the way?"

Every time the boy had answered bravely: —

"Sure, father! Before evening you shall see the palm trees of the oasis, and my mother."

And so it was that just as their horses began to throw long shadows across the sand, suddenly Jamin, who was riding ahead with his father, exclaimed: —

"There they are, father! There are the palm trees! There is my mother!"

And with a wild hurrah he leaned forward, patted Neko's neck, and dashed away over the desert.

With beating heart and fast-coming breath his father followed him. All fear of hostile Arabs — all care, all prudence — he cast to the winds. Hanani had but one thought. Beneath those palm trees was his wife. He must see her! He must reach her! And he followed headlong Jamin in his wild rush onward.

But as he approached the oasis a vague uneasiness seized him. The palm trees waved their plumes more distinctly in the evening air. The velvet green carpet shone beneath their brown trunks. The soft call of birds came to him, but no sign of human inhabitants was here.

As he rode into the oasis, Jamin, who was just before him, threw himself from his horse and turned a white, despairing face toward Hanani.

"Oh, father," he cried, "they are gone! They are gone! My mother! My mother!"

But a moment later the boy stilled his own grief, overwhelmed by the sight of what his father was suffering; for Hanani had thrown himself face downward on the grass, motionless and speechless, in an agony of grief.

The soldiers rode quickly up and gathered around father and son with many exclamations of sympathy and conjectures as to where the Arabs had gone; but they soon discovered that not a clew remained to guide them in a further search. No roads crossed the trackless waste of the desert, and there seemed to be nothing they could do but return to Jerusalem.

CHAPTER XXV

A WEEK had fled since Jamin and his father had set out so joyfully on their search for Hannah and had returned in such great distress.

On that evening, when the little party was seen approaching, Lord Nehe had ridden to meet them, carrying Bani on his horse in front of him. But one look into Jamin's distressed face, as he drew near, told him the story, and without a word he had turned his horse and had ridden back with the little cavalcade, sad and disconsolate, into the city.

Every moment of the governor's time since then had been occupied. How the walls of the city grew, tall, strong, and stately! There was not a break in their continuous length now. And how the Jews worked! The first rays of the morning sun that leaped over Mount Olivet showed crowds of eager men busy with trowel and mortar and hoisting machine, and arrow and spear and shield were ever close at hand. And everywhere Lord Nehe went, clad in a complete suit of burnished brass. With shining helmet and glittering shield, he seemed the very embodiment of the spirit of watchfulness and war.

And when the stars appeared at night, the workers were still there, loth to leave the task on which their hearts were set.

During this week Lord Nehe scarcely saw his mother, and so it was that when one day, his imperious young voice was heard in the corridor of the women's house, demanding the Lady Sarai, she herself drew aside the curtain of her private apartment, and bade him enter. There was no one in the room but a handmaid, busily engaged at an embroidery frame; and, without looking toward her, Nehe turned to the Lady Sarai, catching both her hands in his own.

"What do you think, mother?" he cried gayly; "Sanballat has at last persuaded the king to order us to cease work on the walls. The letter has just arrived by a special messenger. Not another gate is to be set up, not another bolt or bar is to be put in place. The work is to stop — absolutely stop — as soon as I have read this letter."

And he drew from his wallet two burnt bricks, curiously inscribed, which he held out to her.

The Lady Sarai cast a distressed look at her son.

"You are commanded to stop the work, Nehe?" she said, questioningly. "Then why are you so glad?"

An almost boyish laugh broke from Nehe's lips.

"Because the work is finished, mother," he cried. "Every gate has been set up. Every bolt and bar is in place. Strong and broad and mighty, the walls are built around Jerusalem. My mission is accomplished. Our city is safe from its foes!"

Then, raising his head, he looked toward heaven and exclaimed: —

"Remember me, O my God, concerning this, and spare me according to the greatness of thy mercy!"

"Amen," the Lady Sarai said softly, and then she added, "Oh, my son, I can scarcely realize that at last Jerusalem is safe after all these terrible years."

"Safe from those who would enter from without, mother," the young man said, his bright brow clouding. "My great fear now is that enemies may enter through the hearts of the people."

"What do you mean, Nehe?" the Lady Sarai asked anxiously.

"I mean the terrible danger that the Hebrew youths will marry the beautiful heathen girls with whom they are constantly thrown. It will never do, mother," he added passionately; "our only safety lies in separating ourselves from the heathen about us. Did not Solomon, king of Israel, sin on account of these women? Yet among many nations there was no king like him, who was beloved of his God, and God

made him king over all Israel. Nevertheless, even
him did outlandish women cause to sin."

"True, Nehe," Lady Sarai said quietly. "There
was no law kept more carefully by the Jews in captivity than that which forbade them to marry
heathen women."

"Yes," Nehe added meditatively, "that was the
only thing that ever reconciled me to the death of
Lydia. Had she lived, Adna would have wanted to
marry her, and I should not have consented to it.
It would not have been right."

The girl who was seated at the embroidery frame
arose and took a step forward. She threw aside her
veil, and her face shone out like a star.

"My lord," she said, and her voice rang sweet and
clear, "I told you once before, my lord, I did not ask
to marry Adna. I did but ask to love him."

With a cry of almost terrified astonishment Lord
Nehe turned and gazed into the girl's face.

"Lydia!" he exclaimed, "are you living, or is it a
spirit?"

The girl dropped her veil and turned quickly away.

"I am but thy mother's handmaiden Ariel," she
said quietly. "The maiden Lydia, beloved by King
Artaxerxes Longimanus, died and was buried in the
land of Persia. I am but Ariel, my lord."

There was such a depth of sorrow in the girl's words that any thought of reproach died from Lord Nehe's mind, and he turned to his mother, saying: —

"What does it mean, mother? Who is yon maiden? Tell me! I could swear she is Lydia, and yet I know Lydia is dead."

"Best let her so remain, then." Lady Sarai answered. "It were best for her, for you, and for your armor-bearer. With his own arms Adna lifted Lydia's drowned body from the river and carried it to his mother. At the following midnight he returned, and she put into his arms a body closely wrapped in burying clothes. This he laid in the sepulchre of his fathers, and if this body were not that of the maiden Lydia, neither he nor you, nor any other of King Artaxerxes Longimanus's trusted servants, knows to the contrary."

For a moment Lord Nehe stood gazing at Lady Sarai, as if overwhelmed by the words she had spoken. Then he crossed the room and knelt at the feet of the still standing maiden.

"Ariel," he exclaimed reverently, taking her hand and kissing it, "heathen or Hebrew, spirit or maiden, no braver more true heart ever beat in woman's breast."

And rising, he quietly and swiftly walked from the room.

CHAPTER XXVI

IT was the ninth hour of the first day of the seventh month, and the maiden Ariel walked alone in the garden of the governor's palace. It was very unusual for her to be there at that hour, though roses and lilies beckoned her, and birds of bright plumage, like lights thrown from a prism, flashed to and fro among the olive and myrtle trees.

But Ariel had been left alone in the palace, and had endeavored in vain to interest herself in her customary morning occupations. Now, as she moved restlessly about the garden paths, she was fighting some strong impulse. Parting the leaves of a rhododendron bush, she looked into its glossy depths. A thrush lifted its soft eyes and looked fearlessly up at her. As she stood gazing at it, the bird made no motion to stir from the nest on which it was sitting.

As Ariel watched it, a tender, wistful look grew in her blue eyes.

"Birdie," she said softly, "I think it strange, don't you, that the great Lord God who made you, and made me, too, birdie, should have not forgotten you in His laws, and should have forgotten me. See how safely you sit there on your nest, because of

the word He spoke about you so long ago, while I —
I am only a heathen maid, and to-day, in all this
great city, am the only one, save the Persian soldiers,
who may not listen to the reading of His law."

The little bird settled closer on its nest, spreading
its wings with a caressing motion, then looked up
with a glad little chirp. Ariel then saw that the bird
was not watching her, but something beyond her.
Turning, she saw, perched on a branch of an olive
tree above her, the bird's mate, with a ripe mulberry
in its mouth. Ariel drew aside with a little cry.

"And you have a mate, too, birdie," she whispered, "but I," with a little catch in her voice, "I
shall never have one!"

She clasped her little white hands together in mute
distress, and moved on hastily down the garden walk.
A bush of red roses caught her attention, and she
stopped and plucked a full-blown flower. Again she
moved on until she reached the garden-gate. Here
she hesitated a moment, and then, stepping timidly
outside, she gazed at the deserted streets.

"Every one has gone," she said to herself, aloud,
as if seeking comfort in the sound of her own sweet
voice. "It is only five days since Lord Nehe finished
building the walls, and already he is getting the
people ready for the service of the temple."

Just then one of the guards of the palace turned the corner and approached her. Ariel hastily drew her veil, but the man knew, from the fineness of her white linen dress, that she was an inmate of the palace, and the sheen of her golden hair and the grace of her form, that showed even through the folds of her veil, told that she was young.

The soldier lowered his long lance in respectful salute, and was passing on, when Ariel halted him.

"Where are all the inhabitants of Jerusalem to-day?" she asked. "There seems to be none abroad in the streets, nor yet in the houses."

Now the maiden Ariel knew very well where the inhabitants of the city were that day, and she had pleaded long and earnestly to be allowed to join the household of Lord Nehe when they went forth in the morning, but the Lady Sarai had refused to let her accompany them.

"Ariel," she said, "to-day the great scribe Ezra, who has spent years in searching them out, is to read the Jewish laws to the Jews. Thou art but a heathen girl, my child. These laws are not for you."

And Ariel had bowed her head in submission and turned away, but in her heart she was not submissive.

"The God of the Hebrews is my God," she said, "and I would be with His people this day when they learn of His laws."

The rebellious feeling that had taken root in her breast three hours ago had been growing ever since, and now, as she stopped the guard, it was with a wild hope that in some way he might be able to help her to carry out the desire that had taken possession of her.

"All Jerusalem is gathered in the street that is before the water gate, my lady," the soldier answered; "and not the inhabitants of Jerusalem alone, but people from all the surrounding towns are there also. They say that never since the captivity have the Hebrews dared to leave their farms and villages, and come up in a body to Jerusalem, either to keep the feasts or to listen to the reading of the laws. But since my Lord Nehe has built these walls, in two and fifty days, great fear has fallen on all the surrounding nations, and the people have left their homes, without fear of molestation."

"Is it far to the water gate?" Ariel asked timidly.

"It is but a little way," the man answered. "Were not the people listening so attentively to the great scribe, you could almost hear their breathing. Listen to that low, dull murmur! It is the voices of the Levites, repeating the words of Ezra, so that all in the great concourse may hear and understand."

Ariel advanced a step nearer to the soldier, and almost whispered, as she said pleadingly: —

"Could I — could I not join the host that is gathered there? Would any one notice me?"

"Of course you could join them," the man replied good-naturedly. "You are not large enough to attract attention at any time, by your size, I think, my lady; and the Hebrews are too occupied in listening to the reading to notice you to-day. I know not the ways of these Hebrews, but something the great scribe was reading has touched them all strangely, and many a strong man's tears were falling as he listened to the words of that strange scroll. It was time for me to take my place as guard at the palace, else I would not have left, myself."

"Thank you," Ariel said softly, and, turning, she hastened down the narrow, crooked street that led to the water gate.

In a very few minutes she had reached the wide open square that was used by the Jews as their favorite congregating place, and which lay before the water gate. The great square was crowded now with many thousands of people. Fathers and mothers and children were gathered there, dressed in Oriental robes of crimson and purple and blue, and were listening, with eager, painful intentness, to the words that a venerable man was reading to them from a scroll. He was standing on a wooden platform raised high above the heads of the people, at one end of the square. Beside him, on either hand, dressed in their robes of office, stood a body of priests.

He read very slowly and clearly, with long pauses between his sentences, and during these pauses other priests, who were scattered through the vast assemblage, took up the words he had been saying, and repeated them to the crowd about them.

For some time Ariel lingered on the outskirts of the concourse; then, finding that she could hear distinctly, she leaned against one of the pillars at the entrance to the square, and, utterly forgetful of herself, listened intently to the words which fell from the lips of the aged scribe, and which the Levites were repeating.

She scarcely comprehended the words she heard at first, but presently as she listened, she understood that Ezra was reading the directions given by God to the children of Israel when they came into the land of Canaan. Clear and distinct, above the heads of the multitude that lay between her and him, the

words came floating, so clear and distinct, it seemed
as if they were meant for her alone: —

"When the Lord thy God shall bring thee into the
land whither thou goest to possess it, and has cast out
many nations before thee, the Hittites, the Gergas-
hites, and the Amorites," — and Ariel wondered
vaguely to which of these people she belonged, as the
list went on, — "the Canaanites, the Perizzites, and
the Hevites, and the Jebusites, seven nations greater
and mightier than thou; and when the Lord thy God
shall deliver them before thee, thou shalt smite them,
and utterly destroy them; thou shalt make no covenant with them, nor show mercy unto them."

As the scribe's clear, incisive tones fell on her ears,
the girl shuddered, and clung to the pillar for support. She wished with all her heart she had not come.
After all, it had been true kindness on Lady Sarai's
part to try to compel her to remain at home. Her mistress knew what was to be read this day, and would
spare the girl the pain of hearkening to it.

As one who listens to his death sentence, Ariel's eyes
were fixed on the face of the reader, and clearly, slowly,
distinctly, the heart-shattering words went on:—

"Neither shalt thou make marriages with them.
Thy daughter thou shalt not give unto his son, nor
his son shalt thou take unto thy daughter."

With a little moan Ariel sank down at the foot of the pillar, for just as these words were uttered, her fascinated eyes had dropped from the face of the reader to a little group that stood below him on the pavement. There, in all the splendor of his burnished coat of mail, stood Nehe, silent, motionless, erect, his hand resting on his sword and his eyes fastened on the reader. He, too, was drinking in every word of that command, and every line of his vigorous young form showed that here was the power that would enforce those laws.

Beside him stood his armor-bearer, Adna, quiet and sorrowful, yet with the same look of stern determination on his face that rested on that of his master.

At the instant that Ariel discovered him, some sudden impulse caused Adna to shift his gaze from the reader and send a swift glance across the throng. No wonder Ariel sank moaning at the foot of the pillar, for the words of the scribe were ringing in her ears, and the look in Adna's face was flashing in her eyes. For, as he saw her in her white robe, with her golden hair falling about her, and the red rose clasped in her hands, he thought he saw a vision, and when in an instant she disappeared, he was sure of it. And now Ariel crouched trembling at the foot of the pillar, and her tears fell fast, but hers were not the only tears that were falling in that great assemblage. Many a woman was there whose husband had chosen her from among the heathen nations; many a man who had given his son in marriage to a daughter of one of the accursed peoples. But the voices of the scribe and the Levites went steadily on, and at last Ariel hushed her sobs and once more gave her thought to what was being said.

Some of the laws Ezra read were quite clear to her, but others she did not understand; but almost every one that was read seemed to call forth from the people some fresh indication of sorrow.

"I and my house have broken this law," one would say. "What wonder the curse that was threatened came upon us!"

"Little I dreamed that we were disobeying this law," said a handsome man to his wife, standing near Ariel, when the law of the tithes was read.

Consternation and dismay had spread throughout the entire audience, when suddenly Nehemiah, acting in his capacity of Tirshatha, ascended the platform and took his place beside Ezra. Stretching forth his hand to command silence, he looked over the great assembly and said: —

"My people, this day is holy unto the Lord your God. Mourn not nor weep."

There was a world of comfort in his strong, tender young voice; a world of hope and cheer, and many a downcast head was upraised and teardrop wiped away, as men and women turned their faces toward him, as he spoke: —

"Go your way, eat the fat and drink the sweet, and send portions unto them for whom nothing is prepared, for this day is holy unto the Lord. Neither be ye sorry," — and his voice grew strong and deep with a joyousness that sank into the hearts of the people, "for the joy of the Lord is your strength and his mercy is everlasting."

Then Ezra again stepped forward, and raised his hands in benediction, as he said, solemnly and slowly: —

"Peace be within thy walls, O Jerusalem, and prosperity within thy palaces."

"Amen," replied the people, bowing themselves to the ground.

And once again Ezra's voice was heard, as he repeated, in ancient Hebrew, solemnly and slowly, the sweet words that from time immemorial have been the Jews' confession of faith: —

"Hear, O Israel!"

And the people, knowing what was coming, joined with one accord in the words that followed: —

"The Lord our God is one Lord. And thou shalt love the Lord thy God with all thy heart, and with all thy soul, and with all thy might."

Like a mighty chant the words arose toward heaven, and at their sound Ariel, trembling, sprang to her feet. Her heart was beating so fiercely it seemed as if it would suffocate her, and her voice, when she tried to speak, sounded strange and unnatural; but gathering all her courage she struggled to where one of the Levites stood.

The crowd was breaking up now, with sounds of laughter and gladness. Lord Nehe's words of hope and cheer had changed their sorrow into rejoicing, and they were going home to keep the rest of the day in feasting and gladness, as he had bade them. But Ariel scarcely noticed the crowds. Seizing the Levite by the arm, she cried eagerly: —

"Say them again! Say them again! Quick, tell me those words over!"

"What words?" the man asked almost roughly. "Do you think I can repeat in a moment all the words the learned scribe has been studying these thirteen years?"

Then, catching sight of her earnest, excited, pleading face, he said more gently: —

"Which words do you mean, daughter?"

"The last ones," Ariel answered, and she repeated quickly, "The Lord our God is one Lord. And thou shalt love the Lord thy God with all thy heart, and with all thy soul, and with all thy might."

"Why," said the Levite, "what need have I to repeat them? You know the words full well yourself."

"But," questioned Ariel, and a tone of terrible anxiety crept into her voice, "is this the prayer of any other people or of any other nation save that of God's chosen race?"

"God forbid," the Levite answered earnestly. "These are the very words given by the Lord himself to our leader Moses, sacred to every Hebrew, and unknown to any save those born of the seed of Israel."

"Then," said Ariel, lifting her head proudly, with the light of an unutterable joy shining in her blue eyes, "I am a Hebrew! No longer shall my name be called Ariel, but Lydia the Jewess!"

CHAPTER XXVII

A S she spoke, Lydia turned abruptly away. So great, so wonderful, was her joy, its very presence made her dumb. She felt dizzy and faint, and she longed to throw back her veil that she might breathe more freely, but habit held it in place. She clasped her hands over her beating heart, and a sudden revulsion of feeling swept over her. She was never so alive in all her life. There were wings on her feet now, and she fled swiftly along. Her joy clamored for voice. She must tell some one. She must shout aloud. She would have the whole nation know that she belonged to them.

The happy people pushed and jostled her as they hurried through the streets. On every side gladsome greetings were being exchanged. Two old men meeting flung their arms around each other.

"Rejoice, rejoice!" one exclaimed; "once more Jerusalem is builded as a city that is compact together."

And the other answered, sobbing with joy: —

"The Lord has performed His whole work on

Jerusalem. Once more will the Lord of Hosts defend
Jerusalem and Mount Zion."

As Lydia pushed her way through the happy
throng, she caught the fastening of her sandal. The
people were pressing her on every side, so that she
could not stoop to retie it, and, stepping into the
doorway of a house where a sweet-faced woman stood
holding a little child in her arms, she said: —

"My sandal is untied; may I stop to fasten it?"

"Stop and welcome," was the woman's reply.
"This is a glad day in Israel, sister."

"Sister!" How the word thrilled through Lydia's
lonely heart! It seemed to her that she had never
heard anything so sweet, as she answered, gently but
joyfully:—

"A glad day, truly, sister."

As she spoke, she threw back her veil. What
happiness it was to look these Hebrew women in the
face! Never since leaving Persia had she dared to
raise her veil in their presence, for she knew that her
very beauty would render her despicable in their
eyes, for was she not a heathen girl? And her very
fairness might prove a snare to some faithful Jewish
son.

As Lydia's glance lingered on the lady's face, her
heart went out to her. The soft brown eyes into

which she looked were sweetly serious, and on the lady's delicately formed features rested that look of high-born resignation so often found on the faces of Hebrew women. She was clothed in a costly garment of scarlet, however, and Lydia knew, from its handsome embroidery and the richly chased golden ornaments that held it on the shoulders, and the jewels that were hung about her neck and wrists, that the lady belonged to one of the few wealthy families of Jerusalem.

As the stranger caught the sheen of Lydia's golden hair and the glance of her blue eyes, a look of wonder came into her face, and she said, inquiringly: —

"Surely I have not met you before, sister? I know no maiden of your age who belongs to the house of Uzziah and the lineage of David, and yet surely they are your kinsfolk, for the blue of the sky and the yellow of the lily live not in the eyes and the hair of any Hebrews save those of the house of David. Have I not judged aright, sister?"

A flood of color swept over Lydia's fair face.

"I know not," she answered, softly. "I dare not hope that such honor can be mine. I know not my father's house or tribe. I do but know that I am a Hebrew maid returned from the captivity."

"How is that?" the lady asked in a surprised tone.

"It is strange indeed that a Hebrew maid does not know her tribe and lineage, even in captivity."

"I was stolen in my early childhood," Lydia explained, simply, "and I have but this to identify me."

Putting her hand in her bosom, she drew out the ornament which was concealed there. The look of interest deepened in the lady's face as she gazed earnestly at the jewel Lydia held out to her.

"Does this not tell you who you are?" she asked quickly, and without waiting for a reply she took the trinket in her hand, and, touching a spring that Lydia had never found, the ornament opened at the back, disclosing a polished gold surface on which some Hebrew characters were engraved.

The lady turned the writing to the light and scrutinized it eagerly a moment. Then she closed it and handed it back. Her face reflected the radiant look that shone in Lydia's eyes, but her voice trembled with great anxiety as she said softly: —

"Lydia, you were long years a captive in the land of Babylon. Tell me truly, girl, have you bent the knee to false gods? Have you kept the faith of a Hebrew maiden? Better it were to mourn a dead child than live to know an unfaithful daughter."

And Lydia, raising her young head proudly, replied: —

"In the palace of King Artaxerxes Longimanus kept I the faith of the Hebrews, making no prayer save to the Lord God of the Israelites, and living the life of a true Hebrew maiden. That my words are true, you will know if you ask my Lady Sarai, mother of Lord Nehe, Tirshatha of Jerusalem."

The look of joy deepened in the lady's face.

"You are Lydia," she repeated softly, "of the house of Uzziah and of the lineage of David. Enter my house, Lydia, and await the coming of your mother."

With a cry like a sob the girl caught the lady's hands.

"You know my mother!" she gasped. "My mother! And I am of the lineage of David!"

Lydia clasped the lady still more closely, and stood gazing at her a moment. Then, flinging herself upon her neck, the girl broke into convulsive sobs.

"And I thought I was only a heathen girl, despised and rejected of my people! And lo, I am of the lineage of David and of the tribe of Judah! And I, even I, have a living mother!"

The lady held her in her strong arms and soothed her gently.

"You shall see your mother soon, my child," she

said, "for I am her sister, and as soon as a messenger can be sent for her she will be here."

"But I cannot wait!" exclaimed Lydia, impatiently, catching the lady by the hand. "Come, let us hasten to her! My mother, my mother!"

CHAPTER XXVIII

O N the evening of the same day, just before darkness fell over Jerusalem, Lord Nehe entered the temple and knocked at the beautifully carved cedar door that led into the apartments of Ezra the scribe.

It was quickly opened, and Nehe found himself in Ezra's presence. The old man was sitting at a low table, on which, early as it was, a lighted silver lamp had been set. An attendant stood beside him holding in his hand a large roll of parchment, which the scribe was carefully comparing with a similar roll that lay before him on the table. Another silver lamp was suspended from the ceiling, which cast its soft radiance full on the face of the venerable man, bringing out the snowy whiteness of his long hair and beard, and illuminating the stern outlines of his strong yet pure and kindly face.

Nehe stood for an instant gazing at the scribe. The young ruler was clad in a richly embroidered tunic of Tyrian purple, that almost priceless fabric worn only by kings and princes.

As Ezra looked up and met the eyes of Nehe, set in a countenance tanned by desert sun and mountain wind, he thought that he had never seen so handsome a face or so manly and stalwart a form. No shade of envy that he had been deposed to make room for this splendid young man darkened his countenance as he held out his hands affectionately toward him, saying: —

"Welcome, my son! This has been a great day in Jerusalem, and to-morrow will be a still greater one."

"True, my father," Nehe answered respectfully. "I see you are busy, are you not, even now, preparing for it? I came to confer with you on what we shall do."

"We will follow the ancient laws and customs of the feast of tabernacles as closely as may be," Ezra replied. "We will send the people forth into the mount to fetch olive and pine and myrtle branches, and branches of other thick trees, to make booths, as it is written. Then, when the feast is over, we will let them go home and rest awhile, and prepare for the great day of humiliation."

"Have you searched well the records regarding this day also, my father?" Nehe inquired, anxiously.

"Yes," Ezra answered; "for years I have been preparing for just such a time as this, and well I know the programme that should be observed on that day."

"It rightly falls next week, does it not?" Nehe asked.

"It does," the scribe replied. "The tenth day of the seventh month is the time prescribed, but that would scarcely give us time, would it, my lord, to prepare for it?"

"Scarcely," Nehe assented. "Besides, the people will be weary with the feast, and I wish them to be fresh and vigorous when they enter into the new covenant with the Lord. What a wonderful sight that will be," he continued earnestly, his face kindling with enthusiasm, "when two by two we go up into the temple, you and I leading, my father, with the priests and the Levites behind us, and all the princes of the people following in solemn procession, amid the reverential silence of the congregation, to sign that sacred covenant which will give the Israelitish nation the right once more to claim the protection of the Lord God. If the covenant is prepared, may I see it? Are you sure that every word will be pleasing to God and binding on the people?"

"On my knees I have drawn it up," was the answer, "praying day and night that wisdom might be given me. Carefully have I copied the ancient manuscript, letter by letter, word by word, adding nothing, changing nothing. It is a wonderful law, Lord Nehe.

274 WITHIN THE PALACE GATES

How the cruelty of the Persians, the brutality of the Assyrians, the superstitions of the Greeks and the Egyptians, would fade, could they but know this marvellous law! What peace and prosperity might be theirs if they but obeyed it!"

"How easily they could know it," Nehe said, earnestly, "were not their eyes blinded by the worship of false gods. But have you added nothing to the ancient covenant, my father?"

"Nothing," Ezra replied, "save to emphasize the keeping of the Sabbath, the forbidding of marriage with the heathen, and the giving of tithes."

"I have written a prayer myself," Nehe went on hesitatingly; "a prayer of confession and promise. May I read it to you?"

The scribe signified his assent, and Nehe took a small roll of parchment from a silver case, and read aloud that wonderful recital of God's goodness and Israel's transgressions which the Levites offered up on the day of humiliation.

As the rich tones of the reader rang out through the still room, Ezra's face grew more and more soft, and when, toward the close of the petition, the governor's voice faltered, his tears mingled with Nehe's as the reader went on with that matchless confession, that tender, earnest pleading for help: —

"Nevertheless for thy great mercies' sake thou didst not utterly consume them, nor forsake them; for thou art a gracious and merciful God.

"Now therefore, our God, the great, the mighty, and the terrible God, who keepest covenant and mercy, let not all the trouble seem little before thee, that hath come upon us, on our kings, on our princes, and on our priests, and on our prophets, and on our fathers, and on all thy people, since the time of the kings of Assyria unto this day."

At the words, "Let not all the trouble seem little before thee that hath come upon us," Ezra's voice murmured softly: —

"Truly, my lord, it has been very great."

Nehe paused for a moment, and then his strong, tender voice went on with the confession, while Ezra listened silently to the end, though his falling tears manifested his deep appreciation of every word the young ruler was uttering: —

"Howbeit thou art just in all that is brought upon us; for thou hast done right, but we have done wickedly. Neither have our kings, our princes, our priests, nor our fathers, kept thy law, nor hearkened unto thy commandments and thy testimonies, wherewith thou didst testify against them. For they have not served thee in their kingdom, and in thy great goodness that thou gavest them, and in the large and fat land which thou gavest before them, neither turned they from their wicked works.

"Behold, we are servants this day, and for the land that thou gavest unto our fathers to eat the fruit thereof and the good thereof, behold, we are servants in it; and it yieldeth much increase unto the kings whom thou hast set over us because of our sins; also they have dominion over our bodies, and over our cattle, at their pleasure, and we are in great distress.

"And because of all this we make a sure covenant, and write it; and our princes, Levites, and priests, seal unto it."

When he had finished, Nehe stood for a moment in silence. Then Ezra raised his aged hands and laid them softly on the young man's head.

"The Lord bless thee and keep thee," he murmured in a trembling voice. "Surely He hath given thee wisdom from on high to govern and to lead His people."

Bowing low in respectful salutation, Nehe turned and left the scribe's apartment.

Walking rapidly, the young ruler crossed the court of the Israelites, and, passing that of the women, almost stumbled over the figure of a man kneeling in the shadow of a pillar in the court of the Gentiles.

"Who's there?" the governor asked sharply, for the quiet, motionless figure startled him.

The man arose and stepped out of the shadow into the bright moonlight, and then Lord Nehe saw that it was his armor-bearer, Adna.

"What are you doing here?" he demanded. "I have had men searching for you all the afternoon. I have greatly desired you."

"I crave your pardon, my lord," Adna answered, quietly, but with such a strange ring in his voice that Nehe regarded him more closely. "I have seen a vision this day, my lord, and I withdrew from the crowd to think of it."

"What was your vision?" Nehe demanded, imperiously. "This has been a day for rejoicing in Israel, Adna, and not for dreaming."

"I was not dreaming, my lord," Adna replied; "but the vision filled me with a holy joy, and I came here, to the temple of my God, that I might comfort my sad heart with its sweet remembrance."

Lord Nehe had been so utterly absorbed by his conversation with Ezra, and by the strange events of that eventful day, that something which otherwise he would have told Adna on the instant of meeting him had been crowded out of his mind; but as Adna spoke, it came rushing back, and he laid his hand affectionately on his armor-bearer's shoulder, saying: —

"Come, Adna, let us walk home to the palace through the garden, and you shall tell me of your vision, and I will tell you of something more wonderful than any vision, and something that will bring you greater joy."

Adna hesitated a moment, and then the two passed out between the marble columns and down the wide steps of the temple.

"My lord," the armor-bearer said, at length, "I cannot tell you of my vision without confessing to you a sin wherein I have sinned against you. When King Artaxerxes Longimanus, on that dreadful night, sent me to search for Lydia's body, I did not at once call the guard to my assistance, but dashed madly down to the river's brink alone. Scarcely had I reached the water's edge, my lord, when the waves threw her at my very feet. Seizing her instantly, I carried her to my mother's house, and there I laid her on my mother's bed; for it was not meet, my lord, that I should not risk my life to save her sweet dead body, when she had given her life to save my living one. This done, I hastily returned and called the king's guard, and, as you know, we searched all night. Then it was I swore to you that the guard found her not. The next night I went back to my mother's house, thinking to catch one more glimpse of Lydia's lovely face, but my mother had already wrapped her in her winding sheet, and so I could but carry her to my father's sepulchre, and lay her beside him, safe, at least, from the heathen rites and ceremonies of King Artaxerxes Longimanus. Can you forgive me, my lord?"

Nehe took Adna's hand kindly.

"I forgave you long since, Adna," he said. "It is not news you tell me. But was this your vision?"

"Thank you, my lord," Adna replied simply; but his mind was evidently so preoccupied with other thoughts that there was less warmth of gratitude in his voice than there would have been at another time. "And now I will tell you of my vision," he went on, "for it was something real that I saw to-day, and not the dream that I have so often dreamed."

He paused a moment, as if recalling the sight.

"As I stood beside you, while Ezra read aloud the law, and the noise of the weeping of the people and the voices of the Levites rang in my ears, I raised my eyes, and there, standing on a portico leaning against a pillar, dressed in white and holding the same red rose in her hand that she used to hold, her golden hair gleaming around her face like a halo, with parted

lips and shining eyes as she leaned forward, listening
breathlessly, stood Lydia! Then her gaze fell on me,
and her eyes looked straight into mine, with that
same wonderful look of sorrow and love that shone
there when she leaped from the parapet. And then,
as I gazed, she was gone. The pillar shone out white
and bare, the voice of the scribe and the noise of the
people sounded in my ears, but I saw nothing save
Lydia, nor have I seen aught since, my lord. Waking
or sleeping, I shall see her standing there looking at
me, sorrowful and beautiful, until I die."

As they walked, the two young men had reached
the gate of the palace garden. Opening it, they entered. The moonlight fell softly and white on rosebud
and balm tree, on hyacinth and jonquil blossom, and
their perfume was all around them.

"Come, let us sit here," Nehe said, drawing Adna
down upon the gnarled roots of an old olive tree that
spread out dark and black beneath its glossy leaves.
"How beautiful this old garden is to-night, Adna.
Did you ever see the moonlight shine more white?
And how sweet the balm trees are! They say the
Queen of Sheba brought them first to this country,
among her gifts to the mighty King Solomon."

"Was it not strange, my lord," Adna interrupted,
"that Lydia's dress, when I saw her today, was not

such as the Persian maidens wear, but it was fashioned like to those of the Hebrew women? Was it not strange, my lord?"

"Strange indeed," Nehe replied, somewhat impatiently. "But think of this old garden for a moment, Adna. What curious sights this very olive tree may have witnessed! They say that the olive tree counts its life not merely by centuries, but by tens of centuries. Perhaps our father Abraham rested here as he climbed Mount Moriah to offer Isaac on yonder stone that stands now in the temple. Have you seen it, Adna?"

"Yes, my lord," Adna replied listlessly. "It is the great stone on which sacrifice is wont to be made, is it not?"

"The same," Nehe assented dreamily. "I wonder if David and Bathsheba used to walk in this garden and watch the baby Solomon playing among the flowers. I should not be surprised if Solomon himself, in later years, used to bring his lovely Egyptian bride down here to rest awhile in the moonlight. I can fancy her on that first night, sitting beside him here, dressed in her marvellous gown of woven gold, her eyes shining like stars in the darkness, while Solomon sang her that wonderful love song, beseeching her to forget her father's house and to worship him. Ah, if he had only begged her to worship his God, how different might have been his life! But, after all," Nehe added, speaking softly, as if he had forgotten Adna and were communing with himself, "it is not of the past — it is of the future — I think to-night. Who knows but that the great Shiloh Himself will some day rest beneath this olive tree! He will love olive trees, I know! They are so strong and brave and fruitful! O that he might come soon!" he added passionately. "Jerusalem is ready now for her king. The walls are builded, the tribes are returning, the temple is purified. All that man can do to make ready for Him have I done. If only the people have prepared a place for Him in their hearts! For He shall be a holy one when he comes, Adna, and neither prophet nor priest nor king can crown Him, if the people be not ready for Him."

"The whole world awaits His coming, my lord," Adna said respectfully.

"Pray God he may come soon," Nehemiah replied. But I must hasten to tell you the story for which I brought you here, Adna. Can you put your vision out of your mind long enough to listen to it?"

"My vision will never leave me, my lord," Adna answered; "but I will listen to your story."

"Nay, but you must hearken closely," Nehe said,

"for my story may have somewhat to do with your vision. It begins a long way off. In the city of Susa there dwelt among the captive Jews a goldsmith, Uzziah by name. His curious engraving of costly gems had caused him to be in high favor with the king, and he had grown immensely rich. At the time of which I speak, the king had given permission to such of the Hebrews as wished, to return to Jerusalem, and Uzziah decided that he would cast in his lot with those who went back to their own country, knowing that with his wealth he could do much to aid in the rebuilding of the temple. Now this Uzziah had but one child, a fair and beautiful little girl, who was dearer to him than all his riches. She had been in charge of a Persian nurse since her birth, who was very deeply attached to the child. Naturally, when she learned that her charge was to be taken so far away from her as Jerusalem, her grief was intense. Day by day she besought her mistress that she might accompany them, but to this Uzziah would not consent, for the woman was a heathen, and he feared her influence over his daughter as she grew older.

"On the day when Uzziah's caravan set out for Jerusalem, the child and the nurse disappeared. Frantic with grief, the father and mother abandoned their journey and spent a whole year in searching for the missing nurse, but not even a trace of her was ever obtained, and of course no clue of the child. At the end of this time, utterly broken-hearted, Uzziah and his wife went to Jerusalem, and have since spent their lives in doing what they could to succor and help their brethren. Are you listening, Adna?"

"I am listening, my lord," the armor-bearer replied. "My ears hear your words, but my eyes see the vision."

"Oh, foolish eyes," Nehe said, laughing, and laying his hand on Adna's shoulder. "Listen more closely, Adna, for the story grows more interesting. This morning the sister of Uzziah's wife went running to her. 'Come,' she said, 'great joy has fallen to your lot to-day!' And she placed in her arms a beautiful girl, at the same time giving her proof that this maiden was her daughter. Is it not a strange story, Adna?"

"Very strange, my lord," Adna answered listlessly; "but where had the girl been all the time that her father and mother were searching for her?"

"That is the strangest part of it," Lord Nehe went on, and an exultant thrill crept into his voice. "The Persian nurse did not attempt to hide the child. She simply dyed her beautiful golden hair black, and then, going up to the palace of the king, took service

with my lady mother in the harem. No one thought
of searching for the child there. The years passed by,
and the nurse died, leaving the girl to the care of my
mother. But before the Persian woman died she
taught the child a prayer which she said was the
prayer of her own people, and she bound around her
neck a curious ornament which she warned her never
to show to any one until she should hear a congregation recite the prayer aloud. Then she would know
that she had found the people to whom she belonged,
and the ornament would tell them who she was. It
was through that prayer and ornament that the
maiden discovered herself to-day."

"It is an entertaining story, my lord," Adna said,
trying hard to be interested. "And did you say that
the girl returned hither with your mother when we
came from Susa?"

"Yes," Nehe assented, leaning closer toward his
armor-bearer. "Put your vision out of your mind a
moment, Adna. I wish you to hear how. It was ex-
ceedingly strange."

"I am listening, my lord," Adna said patiently;
"but the vision is very present to me. Why, even as I
look down yonder walk, methinks I see the shimmer of
her white garment and the gleam of her golden hair."

Nehe looked in the direction in which Adna

pointed, and then, turning to the young man, resumed hurriedly: —

"Shut your eyes, then, Adna, while I finish this story, for hear it you must. This little girl grew up in the palace of the king, and as she grew, my mother found within her so true a heart, so beautiful a spirit, and so sweet a voice, that she loved her as her own daughter. You know the dangers of the harem, Adna, and my mother, who had taught the maid to worship the God of the Hebrews, shielded her with jealous care, lest the king should look upon her beauty. But one unhappy night, as she loitered singing in the palace garden, King Artaxerxes heard her and sent for her."

"Poor maiden!" Adna exclaimed compassionately. "Then Lydia was not the only one who faced that ordeal, my lord."

Nehe took no notice of the interruption, but continued his narration, speaking rapidly: —

"But when the great king offered her his love and the honor of being his wife, the poor foolish maid spurned him, telling him that her heart was no longer her own. And when the angry monarch still further pressed her, declaring he would discover her lover, the brave girl sprang upon the parapet and from thence plunged into the river."

"My lord!" Adna breathed, bending forward, "my lord! And she died?"

"Oh, no," Nehe said almost carelessly. "Her lover was there in the king's presence. He ran down to the river bank, found her, and took her to his mother."

"But she was dead!" Adna declared, excitedly. "My lord, she was dead! I buried her, my lord! With my own hands I laid her in the sepulchre."

"No, Adna, she was not dead," Nehe asserted. "But your mother knew the fate that would overtake you both were Lydia discovered to be alive, and so she sent her to Jerusalem in the guise of a camel-driver. You have not forgotten Ariel, Adna?"

Casting off Lord Nehe's detaining hand, the armor-bearer sprang to his feet.

"Oh, my lord," he cried, "where is she? Let me go to her!"

Lord Nehe arose, too, and whispered, as he put his hand softly on Adna's arm: —

"Wait! I think she is coming to you."

Adna stood transfixed with emotion. Leaning against the dark trunk of the olive tree, his breath coming in great gasps, he gazed down the path up which a shimmer of white was softly moving; for Lydia, after the great joy of the morning, had longed, as evening came on, for the coming of Adna, and at last, despairing of seeing him that night, had stolen out into the garden, just to be alone for a little while with her great joy — just to say over to herself the things she dared not even think in the crowded palace, with the arms of her father and mother about her; for it seemed ungrateful, when their happiness was so intense, that her heart should turn with such tender longing to another.

As Lydia moved along the walk, suddenly the joy that was in her broke into words, and she approached the two men under the olive tree, singing: —

"I am my beloved's; he whom I love is mine,
The chief among ten thousand, his love to me is wine.
His eyes, like to a dove's eyes, look love into my heart,
And waters cannot quench it, nor floods keep us apart."

The music of Lydia's voice broke the spell that had held Adna motionless, and he sprang forward. The movement startled the girl, who, seeing two dim forms in the darkness, turned to flee.

With a cry of such caressing sweetness that it stopped the fleeing girl as if a strong hand had arrested her, Adna sprang forward: —

"Lydia, my beloved!"

And Lord Nehe, quietly rising, slipped from the garden, his eyes filled with a mist of tender gladness.

CHAPTER XXIX

ON a beautiful morning in early autumn, a party
of Arabs who had encamped on the mountains
of Ephraim came out from their tent and stood looking at the landscape before and around them.

Their camels and horses were tethered near, and
their baggage lay before the door, for it was evident
that these travellers were hastening from Samaria to
the desert, and had drawn aside from the main road,
not only to rest over night, but also to escape observation.

Early as it was, they saw that every road and by-
path was filled with crowds of people hastening toward Jerusalem. From every hamlet and village,
from every terraced vineyard and farm on the sloping
hills, companies of gayly dressed men, women, and
children were issuing. Aged men with white turbans
resting on their still whiter hair, wearing flowing
cloaks of brown and white, walked with their sturdy
sons, whose wives were attired in tunics and shawls
of soft, rich colors. Over their black tresses were
flung the long veils without which a Hebrew woman
was never seen, and often from their folds at the back
peeped out the laughing face of a baby.

These were the matrons, but the younger women wore their veils flung back from their faces, revealing their silver earrings and a multitude of gold and silver chains upon their necks and arms, while other ornaments equally beautiful adorned their slender ankles and dainty feet, making a continual musical sound as the wearers walked. Round about them all flitted the children of the family, their bright-hued garments giving them at a distance the appearance of gorgeous butterflies.

"Surely the hand of God is with this people," one of the Arabs said. "Look at yonder hillside. The ancient terraces are all occupied again, and soon orchards of olive and walnut, fig and pomegranate trees, will climb their sides to the very top, as they did in the days of the great King Solomon."

As the Arabs looked, the gates of the small walled town of Geba opened, and a procession issued forth. Although the observers on their mountain perch were high above the village, they could see that the company was composed of stalwart youths and men dressed in flowing white garments. As the procession poured forth from the gate, the men took up a long, swinging, steady stride, and through the sweet, clear morning air came a burst of deepest melody: —

"Make a joyful noise unto the Lord, all ye lands!"

The words floated up clear and distinct, and the Arabs hushed their speech to listen; but in a moment one said: —

"Those are the singers that are to sing to-day at the great festivity, when the young ruler dedicates the mighty walls of Jerusalem. See, yonder comes another band."

As he spoke, a procession similar to the first issued from Azmaveth, a city set like a pearl in the emerald of the fields below. This second company, catching the words the first was singing, joined its voices with those of their brethren, and a flood of melody went sweeping up the hillsides as the psalm of praise went on: —

"Serve the Lord with gladness; come before his presence with singing."

Then valley and hillside were filled with music and rejoicing, for other companies of singers and parties of white-robed Levites took up the song, while many families, as they journeyed onward, added their voices to the psalm, the shrill tones of the women, accompanied by the tinkling of their silver ornaments, rising high and clear above the deep bass of the men.

"There will be no one left on hillside or plain to-day," a young Arab said, turning to an elderly man who just then came out of the tent. "What a day this would be for raiding flocks and herds."

"Think not of it, my son, I pray you," the old man answered. "Since the Hebrews have rebuilt the walls of Jerusalem, 'tis said that the mighty God who protected King Solomon has again come to the aid of this people."

"Nevertheless," the son insisted, "you will not give up your errand in the city, will you, O sheik?"

"No," the old man replied; "we will continue our undertaking. 'Tis true I failed to sell the woman to Sanballat, but I do not despair of getting back the mare."

"I wonder," the young man said hesitatingly, "if it would not be better to try to buy Neko back? I put no trust in the stables' being left unguarded to-day."

"Has your heart melted, my son?" the old man asked scornfully. "If so, I will myself go for the mare."

"Fear has no lodgement in my bosom," the young man replied proudly; "but see, the people are fast entering Jerusalem. It is time we set forth."

As they turned away, the old man stopped to speak a word of warning to the tribesmen who were lingering near the tent door.

"Guard well the woman," he commanded. "Let no man see her face; it was in this neighborhood she was made captive. Be quite ready to start, but do not leave this spot until you see my son ride out of the Damascus gate on the mare. Then do not attempt to follow him, but strike straight for our tribe in the desert. I will join you on the road."

Then, girding up their robes, father and son set out toward Jerusalem, the sheik riding a horse, while his son walked beside him.

An hour's journey brought the Arabs to the gate, and as they approached it, their progress became more and more difficult. Crowds of people pressed them on every side, for the whole population of the surrounding country was hastening to reach Jerusalem before the hour set for the dedication of the walls.

Once inside the gate, the pushing, jostling crowd divided. The women and children, and part of the men, with the servants and the aged, hastened to the large open space in front of the temple, while the priests and the Levites, the singers, the princes of Judah and Benjamin, and the heads of families who were to take part in the dedication ceremonies, made their way as rapidly as possible to the western wall, from whence the procession was to start. Here marshals were awaiting them, ready to show every man the place assigned him. So quietly and quickly was this work done, that when the sun-dial marked the hour of nine, a long flourish of trumpets proclaimed to the waiting people that the procession was about to move.

Four abreast the singers marched up the steps to the top of the wall, and then divided into two companies, one of which turned to the south and the other to the north. To the waiting throngs below, watching the procession, the sight was one that aroused their deepest enthusiasm and patriotism.

The singers led the way, their marching figures silhouetted against the blue of the sky, as with pipe and harp, psaltery and sackbut, they raised the mighty chant: —

"They that trust in the Lord shall be as Mount Zion, which cannot be removed, but abideth forever."

And lifting up their eyes to the hills, the chorus came back: —

"As the mountains are round about Jerusalem, so the Lord is round about his people from henceforth even forever."

As the singers ascended the wall, they were followed by Lord Nehe and Ezra, clad alike in the long, white garments of the scribes. The stature, as well as the garments of the two, was the same, but here all similarity in their appearance ceased. Ezra's white head was bent with the weight of many years of incessant toil and disappointment, and on his stern features rested a look of sweet and touching resignation that even the proud triumph of to-day could not dispel. As he glanced at the body of singers already pouring forth their floods of joyous song, he compared their number with that of the four thousand that had taken part in the dedication of the first great temple, and he sighed for Israel's lost glory.

But Nehemiah carried his head proudly, and on his face rested a look of glad and triumphant sweetness. The work that he had set out to do had been accomplished infinitely better than he had dared to hope. He thought not of Israel's vanished greatness, but of her promised glory; and in the bands of singing men and marching princes he saw dimly foreshadowed the great army that should some day follow the Prince of Peace.

Behind the leaders marched the dignitaries of the city, clad in their magnificent robes, rich in every brilliant hue dear to the Oriental heart, and contrasting with the white robes of the singers who preceded them and of the priestly families that followed. Seen from a distance, they looked as if a gigantic rainbow had been torn from its place in the heavens and stretched along the ramparts of Jerusalem.

Leaning on their staves came next the princes of the people, and back of all another company of white-robed priests, shrilling forth their joy on silver trumpets, the sign of their sacred office.

Solemnly and majestically, the two bands, in charge of their respective leaders, Nehemiah and Ezra, circled the city walls, going in opposite directions, voice answering to voice, and trumpet call to trumpet call, until at last they faced each other in the prison gate, and, joining their forces, swept down from the wall. The waiting throng caught up the song, men, women, and children uniting their voices to those of the musicians. High and loud the melody rose, until it seemed that the very skies themselves joined in the singing, so clear and sweet, so strong and triumphant it was. As the great host went rejoicing up the steps into the temple, the magnificent chorus chanted, "For He is good, for His mercy endureth forever." And Lord Nehe raised his proud, wistful young eyes, half hoping, half expecting, that the strange, mysterious golden cloud which had once proclaimed God's presence, would again fill the temple.

CHAPTER XXX

IT was late in the afternoon when Lord Nehe and Hanani entered the private apartment of their mother. Lady Sarai came forward and greeted them affectionately, and little Bani, who was trying to tie a tinkling bell to the neck of a tiny fawn, dropped his toy and sprang into his father's arms.

But Jamin, who was standing by a window watching the sun as it threw a flood of golden light over the joyous city, turned an eager, strained face upon his uncle, but did not leave his post.

"Come hither, Jamin," Hanani cried. "Have you no welcome for your father to-night? See, little Bani has seized the first kiss, and it is your birthright, my son."

Jamin obediently moved forward, but his eyes looked appealingly into Lord Nehe's face.

"Uncle," he cried, "will the sun never set to-night? All the afternoon I have lain beside the dial watching, and for hours sometimes the shadow has not moved. And now see the sun, it hangs there like a great red flower thrown against the sky. It has no life or motion. Will it never set again?"

Hanani looked at the boy anxiously, and laid a caressing hand on his hot forehead.

"Are you ill, Jamin?" he asked tenderly. "Usually the sun sinks all too fast for you boys. What is the matter to-night?"

Before Jamin could answer, Lord Nehe put out his hand and drew the excited boy to him. Bending his head he whispered softly in his ear. As Jamin heard the words and felt his uncle's strong, tender clasp, his face lost its anxious look and one of wonderful brightness took its place; but again his eyes sought the window from which he could see the sun flinging great waves of crimson light across the sky.

"What a wonderful day this has been!" Hanani exclaimed, turning again to Lord Nehe, as he seated himself and lifted little Bani to his knee. "But my heart fails me when I think of governing so great a people. I pray that Artaxerxes may soon permit you to return to Jerusalem. Must you indeed set out for Susa next month?"

"I must indeed," Nehe answered. "The king's order was imperative. Do you but follow the law, Hanani, and all will be well with the people."

"I will try," Hanani replied quietly. "If but this ceaseless pain that gnaws at my heart could have ease, methinks I could be a better and wiser judge."

At this moment an attendant entered, and, going swiftly to Lord Nehe, spoke to him in a low voice. Jamin leaned forward eagerly to catch the words. Then with a cry he sprang up, seized little Bani by the hand, and rushed from the room. Lady Sarai glanced up with a startled look, and Lord Nehe arose and stood before his brother with a look of happiness on his face.

"Your pain shall have a speedy relief, Hanani," he said, with the same joyous ring in his voice that had been there the night he found his brother in the far-away garden in Susa.

Hanani leaped to his feet excitedly, and Nehe went on: —

"To-day as I sat in my room after the ceremony in the temple, word was brought that a messenger from Sanballat awaited me. 'I will not see him!' I cried in sudden fury. 'Perchance he comes, as he came before, with another open letter from Sanballat, the greatest insult one ruler can offer to another. He would degrade and humiliate me in the sight of my people. Drive the fellow hence, with blows if need be, for I will not see him.'

"The attendant went out, and in a moment Jamin, who had just left me after telling a strange tale of how he had seen Sheik Imbrim in the crowd this

morning, came flying back with news that made me
send instantly after the departing man.

"When the messenger was brought into my apartment, one of my soldiers whispered to me that he had
seen the man with an Arab who had made a vain
attempt to steal the mare Neko from her stall while
the dedication ceremonies were in progress. I turned
to the man and asked him what his business might be.
Bowing low, he told me that he had been sent by Sanballat to tell me that the son of one of his slaves had
stolen from him a mare that was valuable to him because he had raised her and feared not to ride her,
but to others the horse was vicious and not to be
trusted. This horse, he had heard, was now in my
stable in Jerusalem. 'Justice and right,' the sheik
continued, 'demand that the mare be returned to her
owner; but the generous Sanballat has sent you rich
presents in exchange for his favorite steed. So a man
awaits without, with a carpet of priceless value, and
gold the worth of many a slave.'

"Then I arose in my wrath and plucked him by
the beard. 'Thou liest, Sheik Imbrim,' I said; 'the
horse is thine own and not Sanballat's. Thou didst
try but this morning to steal her from my stables.
And the boy who took her is no slave, but the son of
the man who was to-day made governor of Jeru-

salem, to rule during my absence. Moreover, thou holdest now in thy possession Hannah, this man's beautiful wife.'

"'By the sepulchre of my fathers,' he declared, 'some one hath deceived my lord. I know not the woman.'

"'By the sepulchre of my fathers,' I retorted, 'thou shalt die this night if Hannah be not brought here as soon as swiftest horse and fastest rider can bring her.'

"Then I called Jamin from where he was hidden in the archway of the door. When the sheik saw him, he fell down at my feet and confessed that his story was a lie and that he told it thinking I would more readily grant the request of a great chief than that of an unknown Arab sheik.

"'I will arise and bring the woman hither at once,' he said, 'for she is near at hand in the mountains.'

"But this I refused to permit, and sent out for the messenger who had carried in the carpet. 'Now take Sheik Imbrim's signet ring,' I commanded him, 'and the gold thou hast brought and the carpet, and haste thee to the mountains. Return speedily with the woman Hannah, who is held captive. And mark thee well! Now the sun rides high in the heavens. If Hannah be not here when he has sunk behind yon hills, Sheik Imbrim dies! For many and grievous are the troubles he has brought upon my people, and well he deserves this punishment.'"

With white face and trembling lips Hanani had been listening in an agony of suspense to Lord Nehe's words. Now he could restrain himself no longer.

"Oh, Nehe," he cried, "why did you not send me? I would have found her and she would have been here hours ago."

"It was not meet," Nehe answered quietly, "that when this afternoon was set as the time to present you to the people as their future governor, you should be absent. The king's business cannot wait, my brother."

"But did you leave my wife in the hands of the Arabs?" Hanani demanded.

"No, dear brother," Nehe replied. "I sent Adna with a mounted guard of my best Persian soldiers, and he swore to me that he would be back with Hannah before the sun should set."

With a common impulse the brothers turned to the open window, while Lady Sarai, the soft tears flooding her eyes, fell on her knees with her face upraised toward heaven, in silent supplication.

The sun hung like a red globe low in the sky, and then suddenly, swiftly, as if pushed by mighty, merciful, unseen hands, it sank behind the horizon and was gone.

Hanani turned to Nehe and grasped both his arms.

"The sunset has come and gone," he gasped; "where is Hannah, my wife?"

"I am here, beloved," a sweet voice answered, and, turning, Hanani saw her standing in the open doorway. Framed in its marble purity, with the glory of the crimson sunset flooding her white garments, she looked as if carved from alabaster. One strong, shapely arm held Bani tightly pressed against her bosom, his golden curls mingling with her down-falling black tresses. With her other arm she circled Jamin, but her eyes were on her husband's face alone, and as Hanani looked deep into their shining depths, a wave of perfect happiness swept over him.

In an instant he had caught Hannah in his arms, and all the joy of that great city could not equal the joy in that little room.

CHAPTER XXXI

A MONTH has passed since the walls of Jerusalem were dedicated, and once again the morning sun, flooding the city with the splendor of a new day, shows crowds of hurrying people filling its streets.

But to-day there is no gorgeous procession for them to see. There is no blare of trumpets nor sound of drums, and when the people greet each other it is with hushed voices and saddened faces.

The way from the palace to the water gate is lined with the waiting crowd. Many tears are falling as the people turn toward the palace. Presently its gate opens and there issues forth a little procession. It consists of a few score splendidly equipped soldiers, dressed from head to foot in Persian armor and mounted upon fine, swiftly moving steeds. The men carry the shining gilded shields borne only by the king's guard. Behind them come the dromedaries, rapid and silent as shadows, loaded with camp utensils, and back of them more soldiers.

At the head of the cavalcade, clad in the glittering suit of armor so familiar and so dear to the eyes of the inhabitants of Jerusalem, rides their loved young ruler, Lord Nehemiah. As he moves swiftly down the street, with pale, set face and shining eyes, many a hand is outstretched toward him in blessing and affectionate farewell.

The people press against the sides of the narrow streets as the cavalcade passes swiftly by, but Lord Nehe pauses not. With jingle of spurs and clink of armor the company rides steadily toward the gate. The great square before it is densely packed with the thronging crowds, and here, as in the streets, prayers and sobs and blessings greet the young ruler as he pauses for a moment while the heavy bolts and bars of the gate are being withdrawn.

As Nehe faces the waiting people, a tall Levite, raising his voice above the murmur of the multitude, stretches out both arms toward him and calls beseechingly: —

"When thou standest in the palace of the king, my lord, forget us not. Return, O well beloved; return to us again!"

With his left hand Lord Nehe raises his helmet, as he extends his right toward the weeping multitude, while his voice rings clear and sweet as the call of a silver trumpet: —

"If I forget thee, O Jerusalem, let my right hand

forget her cunning! Let my tongue cleave to the roof of my mouth if I prefer not Jerusalem above my chief joy!"

As he finishes speaking, the beautiful Miriam, standing by Shallum her father, springs forward and throws around the neck of Lord Nehe's charger a garland of white roses. Leaning forward, Nehe selects one of the blossoms and thrusts it between the links of his armor over his heart. With tear-dimmed eyes the young ruler once more bends his head in silent salutation. The tears and sobs break out afresh. The gate flies open with a clang. The cavalcade passes through, the gate is closed behind it, and the people realize that their loved governor is gone.

For a time the party gallops swiftly along the road, and as Nehe rides, the set look leaves his face and is replaced by one of deep and happy interest. Wherever he turns, signs of prosperity greet him. As he descends the valley, shepherds are seen leading forth their flocks, herds of cattle are grazing on the hillsides, and the smoke ascending from the hearths of hundreds of farms and villages tells that the inhabitants are preparing their morning meal in peace and quietness. In the plains below, fields of grain stretch away on every hand, and the odor of balm trees and the scent of fragrant vineyards fill the morning air.

At length the band reaches the height of Olivet, and turns to descend the eastern slope. Here Lord Nehe halts his horse and lets his troop sweep past him. When it is quite gone, he faces about and once more views the land for which he has suffered and has dared so much.

Terrace above terrace, height above height, as far as the eye can see, stretch the green hills toward the north, while on the south the mountains of Moab drop like a purple veil, shutting out the sands of the desert. Before him, far away, shines the great sea, the silver shield that God has set between His people and the barbarians. Beneath him, so near in the clear morning air it seems as if it lay at his very feet, is Jerusalem! And as he sits there, motionless and silent, his eyes rest on the city in an ecstasy of delight. How magnificent it is, throned like a queen on the hill of Zion, with her mighty walls, like strong arms, encircling her, and her glorious temple, pure and white, gleaming like a precious pearl, crowning her right royally.

For a moment more Lord Nehe gazes in silence. Then, stretching forth both arms, as though he would enfold the city, he exclaims: —

"How beautiful thou art, O Jerusalem! Peace be within thy walls, and prosperity within thy palaces!"

Then, clasping his hands and raising them reverently toward heaven, he exclaims entreatingly: —

"Think upon me, my God, for good, according to all that I have done for this people."

Again he casts a long, lingering look upon the city, brooding over it as a mother broods over the face of her sleeping babe. Then, turning his horse abruptly, he disappears down the mountain pass.